# SECRETS *of* MAGIC

# SECRETS *of* MAGIC

*by*

## WALTER GIBSON

*Illustrated by*

### KYUZO TSUGAMI

*GROSSET & DUNLAP*
PUBLISHERS   NEW YORK

# Contents

# SECRETS *of* MAGIC

# PART 1

# *The* SECRETS
# *of the* ANCIENTS

## Introduction

From the dawn of time, the lure of magic has been felt by men of every race and clime. Man's awe of natural forces and the unknown inspired a trust that self-appointed wonder workers soon turned to their own advantage. Whether they really believed they had special powers or whether they dealt in deliberate deception, their purpose was to win profit or prestige through the admiration of the populace.

These early magicians were the scientists of their time. They regarded their closely guarded secrets as a form of true magic. Whenever they used outright trickery their hope was to thereby strengthen their reputations as purveyors of the genuinely miraculous. If they believed in their own magic, it was because they shared the ignorance of the people who accepted illusion for reality.

Ancient Egypt developed the highest civilization of its day, so it is not surprising that the earliest recorded story of magic should concern the performance of an Egyptian magician, Tchatcha-em-ankh, at the court of King Khufu in the year 3766 B.C. This is recorded in the Westcar papyrus, which dates back to 1550 B.C. and is preserved in the British Museum.

# Ancient Egyptian Marvels

According to the papyrus, Tchatcha-em-ankh knew the number of stars in the House of Thoth, made a lion follow him as if led by a rope, and could bind on a head that had been cut off. The first of these refers to his knowledge of astronomy and astrology, which were closely related in ancient times, while the other two were feats of sheer wizardry.

To make the lion follow him as if led, Tchatcha-em-ankh undoubtedly hypnotized the beast before releasing it. The performance itself is not so remarkable as the fact that hypnotism was so well understood and practically applied at such an early date. More than 5,000 years later, A.D. 1841, a Swiss mesmerist named Lafontaine created a sensation by hypnotizing a lion in the London Zoo. His supposedly modern skill in "animal magnetism," as it was then styled, probably no more than duplicated the ancient demonstration given by Tchatcha-em-ankh.

The restoring of a cut-off head was another ancient marvel that has its modern counterparts. This was obviously a decapitation trick, in which the pretended victim "returns" to life. In the 1920's, during a legal controversy over a modern illusion of "sawing a woman in half," the Westcar papyrus was introduced as evidence that the secret had been known more than 5,000 years earlier.

Though the papyrus does not delve into the actual method, it furnishes clues to the decapitation mystery by describing the performance of a later magician, Deda, who worked along similar lines. Deda presented the decapitation mystery, not with a human subject, but with ducks, geese, even an ox, as occasion might demand. With a duck or a goose, the trick is easily explained, for it has often been worked by modern magicians as a comedy stunt.

Deda's procedure must have been as follows: In pretending to wrench or cut a duck's head from its body, he simply tucked its head beneath its wing and with the same action adroitly brought a dummy head from the fold of his robe. This he exhibited as the original. Later, to restore the bird to life, he reversed the process, slipping the fake head beneath his robe under cover of the duck's body and bringing the real head from under the duck's wing.

Deda could also work the restoration from

a distance, slipping the head beneath his robe while an assistant, who held the duck, gave it a slight toss that brought its real head into sight. Many such tricks may be performed with fowls, for they are also easily "hypnotized" by bending their heads down and drawing a lengthwise line in front of their eyes.

As for the decapitation of an ox, Deda might have chopped off a dummy head at the start, turning the animal so that its real head was lowered from sight. The ox being a dumb and patient beast, it could easily be made a party to such deception. More likely, Deda never performed the decapitation of an ox, but merely claimed that he could do so, citing his success with ducks and geese as proof of his powers.

Exaggeration has been a stock-in-trade of wonder workers from ancient times to the present, so it must be taken into consideration. Only by checking recorded descriptions against known methods can marvels be properly appraised, as they will be in the pages that follow.

# Pharaoh's Serpents

Another link between the sorcery of ancient Egypt and the wizardry of a later era dates back to the Biblical account of the duel between Aaron and Pharaoh's sorcerers. When Aaron cast down his rod, it became a serpent; and when the Egyptian magicians did likewise, Aaron's serpent swallowed theirs.

The account specifically states that the Egyptians utilized their own "enchantments" and "secrets." Hence the serpent mystery was apparently a standard item among Egyptian sorcerers, rather than a specialty of Jannes and Jambres, the two wizards who contested unsuccessfully with Aaron. In that case, it would logically have been carried down through the courts of successive pharaohs, and later spread among itinerant wonder workers.

The facts point to that very result, for there are reliable reports of modern Egyptian wizards who have performed a similar trick. The magician takes a short stick and throws it on the ground, where it wriggles slowly away, causing consternation among the onlookers when they realize that it has become a live snake.

Actually, the stick is a snake at the very start. The trick depends upon a species called the *naja haje*, or the Egyptian cobra. A peculiarity of this snake is that it can be made motionless by pressure just below the head. Thus temporarily paralyzed, the *naja haje* becomes rigid, like a stick, but when it is thrown on the ground, it is jolted back to action.

Photographs have been taken showing how closely the rigid snake resembles a stick, and instances have been reported where modern Egyptian magicians allow bystanders to handle "charmed" snakes with impunity. All this forms a link with the ancient wizardry that flourished under the rule of the pharaohs.

Ancient sorcerers who performed the trick probably carried staffs of similar size and shape to the rigid *naja haje*. By substituting a paralyzed snake at the proper time, it could still be shown as an ordinary stick up to the moment when it was thrown to the ground.

# The Statue of Memnon

Across the river Nile from Karnak are two massive stone statues, each nearly seventy feet high. These are seated figures of the same Pharaoh, Amenhotep III, who ruled Egypt in 1400 B.C., and they marked the entrance to his temple, long since vanished. Although they are identical in appearance, the one on the right has been credited with magical power

that has continued at intervals through the centuries. Every morning, at dawn, it uttered a strange, unexplainable cry as a greeting to the rising sun.

Presumably, this began during the brief period when the Egyptians worshipped the sun under the name of Aton, referring to the solar disk itself. But the cry persisted long

14

after that, and when Cambyses, King of Persia, conquered Egypt in 525 B.C., he supposedly broke and overturned the statue to put an end to its mysterious utterances. Another account attributes the demolition of the vocal statue to an earthquake, but both versions agree that after the statue was restored—though mutilated—it resumed its morning call.

Later, when Grecian influence became strong in Egypt, the statue was identified as representing Memnon, the son of Eos, goddess of the dawn, to whom he gave his cry of greeting. Most important, this call continued until A.D. 200, and was heard and reported by many famous personages, including the historians Strabo and Pliny, the renowned traveler Pausanias, and the Roman emperor Hadrian. Many notable visitors inscribed their names on the base of the statue, stating in Greek or Latin the time at which they had heard the mysterious cry.

Descriptions of the sound varied. Some heard the twang of a harp-string, while others reported hearing the clang of a hammer on metal, or even a spoken word. The cry came from the base rather than the statue itself; in fact, the sounds were heard at a time when the upper half of the statue was lying on the ground. This led to the theory that there was a secret entrance to the base, where Egyptian priests, at different periods, were hidden at dawn and produced the odd sound to awe the populace.

This is hardly plausible, considering that the phenomenon continued through many centuries, despite changes of time and custom. A better explanation was offered by a Frenchman named Dussault, who claimed that since the statue was hollow, the heat of the rising sun warmed the air which it contained; and the air, issuing through cracks in the granite, produced the occasional sounds which were variously interpreted by the persons who heard them.

Later investigators agreed that Dussault was correct insofar as the sun's effect on the granite was concerned. Sir David Brewster cites cases where similar sounds were heard from rock formations, both in Egypt and elsewhere, apparently produced by the heat of the sun.

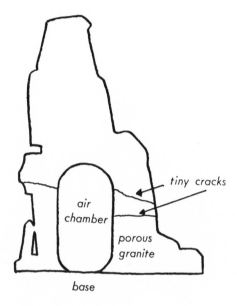

base

Therefore, the question is: Was the statue of Memnon constructed from such rock by accident or by design? Either way, the mystery can be classed as a natural phenomenon rather than outright trickery.

This was partially confirmed around A.D. 1820, when a party of English investigators claimed to have heard the sound again. This was some sixteen centuries after the statue had gone silent following repairs made during the reign of the Roman emperor Septimus Severus. This chance recurrence naturally ruled out any fakery on the part of ancient Egyptian priests or wonder workers, as their era had long since passed.

During the last century and a half, however, the famed statue has maintained a strict silence. So the challenge of the centuries still stands, and tourists who travel up the Nile today may view the mighty monolith of Memnon and solve its riddle—if they can!

# The Idol of Bel

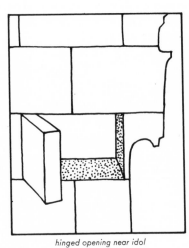

*hinged opening near idol*

Intriguing insight into the ways and wiles of ancient wonders is found in the Biblical account of the prophet Daniel's encounter with the priests of Bel, the great Babylonian idol. The statue of Bel was housed in its own special temple; and to prove it was a living deity, vast amounts of food and drink were placed before the idol every night. The doors of the temple were then closed, and by morn-ing the idol had devoured the entire meal consisting of twelve measures of flour, forty sheep, and sixty vessels of wine.

Through this apparent miracle, the priests of Bel maintained their prestige and won over Cyrus, the Persian king, to the worship of the Babylonian idol. However, when Cyrus demanded that Daniel join him in worshipping Bel, the prophet countered that no mere statue of brass and clay could possibly eat or drink.

The priests of Bel were equal to that challenge. They insisted that the king have his own servants spread the food and drink before Bel; and upon leaving, the king himself should affix his own seal upon the door of the temple so that no one could enter without a trace. Cyrus agreed to this, and after dismissing the priests of Bel, he and Daniel superintended the placement of the food and the sealing of the door.

Morning came, the temple was opened, and the food was completely gone. When Cyrus saw the bare table, he was ready to rush in and worship Bel, but Daniel restrained him. From the doorway, Daniel pointed out evidence of another sort, a multitude of footprints leading from the idol to the temple walls.

The night before, Daniel had secretly brought in containers filled with fine ashes, along with the food and wine. While servants were spreading Bel's repast, Daniel had others sift the ashes all about the idol. The siftings were too fine to be noticed in the dimly lighted temple by the priests of Bel, who entered by secret openings in the walls, bringing their wives and children to enjoy their nightly feast at the expense of their dupe, King Cyrus.

There were seventy priests of Bel; these, together with their families totaled several hundred, accounting for Bel's tremendous appetite. Possibly Daniel calculated that beforehand. In any event, the disclosure spelled doom for the priests of Bel. Cyrus disposed of them and their families, and turned over to Daniel the destruction of the idol and the demolition of the temple as his reward for exposing the fraud.

# The Tomb of Belus

When Xerxes, King of Persia, began his conquest of the ancient world around 480 B.C., he came upon a temple containing the tomb of a legendary king named Belus, which was said to be part of the famous Tower of Babel. Finding some great golden statues in the temple, Xerxes decided to plunder the tomb as well.

Within, the body of Belus was discovered in a coffin only partly filled with oil. Upon the coffin was this inscription: "Woe unto him who violates this tomb and does not complete the filling of it."

The ominous message preyed upon Xerxes' mind, and he ordered that the coffin be filled with oil. It was done, but a few hours after the filling, the oil had mysteriously returned to its original level. Again the coffin was filled, and during the process, no leakage could be discovered; but once more the oil sank to the same level.

Rather than ruin the tomb in searching for the explanation of the mystery, Xerxes commanded that the tomb be sealed, as it had been found originally. Then the Persians set forth on further conquests. The omen was fulfilled, however, for the Persian hosts were overthrown by the Greeks, and Xerxes' power was broken. This strange story was recorded by an ancient historian, and later discoveries have solved the mystery.

Had the tomb contained merely an outlet there would have been no mystery attached to it, for the oil would have flowed out as fast as it was poured in, and the Persians would have discovered the secret easily. The source of the mystery was far more subtle.

It depended upon the application of the principle of the siphon. Concealed in the ornamentation inside the tomb was a small outlet, as illustrated in the diagram. From this opening a curved tube ran upward and through the wall of the tomb, almost to the top, then descended to a hidden, subterranean reservoir.

The tomb was filled with oil just a little above the opening, covering it from searching eyes. The curved bend in the tube prevented the oil from escaping.

When the Persians opened the tomb and examined it, they saw that it was not completely filled. They poured in more oil and raised the level, forcing it up and up in the outlet tube. Eventually the oil reached the curved part of the tube. As more and more oil was poured in, it rose over the bend and began to flow out, forming a siphon-like device. From the tomb the oil slowly began to pass into the hidden reservoir.

So long as there was atmospheric pressure and no air could get into the tube, the liquid continued to flow. When the oil in the tomb dropped just enough below the opening of the tube to allow air to enter, the continuous flow was broken. An air pocket formed at the bend of the tube, and the flow of oil ceased. Some of it even flowed back into the tomb and covered up the opening again.

Since the tube and the whole simple device passed through the stone, it was impossible to solve the secret purely on general knowledge of the science of the time without demolishing the vault itself.

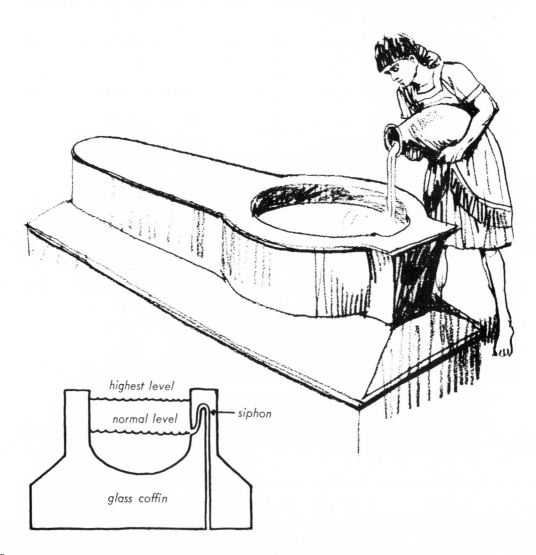

highest level

normal level — siphon

glass coffin

18

# The Temple of Thunder

Remarkable devices were installed in the ancient temples. So far as the ignorant populace was concerned, these bordered on the miraculous. Some accounts are so fanciful that it is difficult to credit them, but in others the marvels can be traced through various stages of development and explained.

The famous labyrinth at Crocodilopolis, near Lake Moeris in ancient Egypt, provides a striking example. It was visited about 450 B.C. by the Greek historian Herodotus, who declared it a wonder surpassing the pyramids, and added that if all the great works of the Greeks were put together in one, they would

19

not equal the Egyptian labyrinth in labor or expense.

Herodotus was personally conducted through 1,500 upper chambers which included twelve roofed palaces, with varied windings and intricate passages. He was not admitted to the subterranean chambers, which were the sacred precincts of dead kings and living crocodiles. Exquisite as the chambers were, Herodotus made no miraculous reports concerning them, though he was usually quick to seize on such rumors or claims.

However, the Roman naturalist Pliny, describing the same labyrinth 500 years later, about A.D. 50, amplified Herodotus' account. According to Sir David Brewster, "Pliny, in whose time this singular structure existed, informs us that some of the palaces were so constructed that their doors could not be opened without permitting peals of thunder to be heard in the interior." These thunderous sounds were attributed to the Egyptian gods, who had apparently taken control since the time of Herodotus, or he would have mentioned them.

Evidently, something new had been added to the Egyptian labyrinth. The explanation is found in the writings of Hero, or Heron, an Alexandrian mathematician, which date from about 150 B.C. Hero described the inventions of his predecessors in chronological order and concluded with some of his own. In the earlier section of his work he wrote of a temple door which gave forth a thunderous blast whenever it was opened, much to the awe of persons about to enter, and gave a detailed description of the automatic device that produced this phenomenon. Attached to the door was a cord or chain, as shown in the explanatory diagram. The cord ran over pulleys and connected with a lever attached to a trumpet, which had a hollow half of a large brass ball in place of the ordinary mouthpiece.

Opening the door loosened the chain and lowered the half-ball into a container of water. The air in the hemisphere was forced through the trumpet, causing a loud blast. From Hero's account, this was probably a stock item in many pagan temples. The effect of several such devices, operating simultaneously or in succession, can well be imagined on the lavish scale of the Egyptian labyrinth. Their thunder would be magnified in proportion to the size and number of doors.

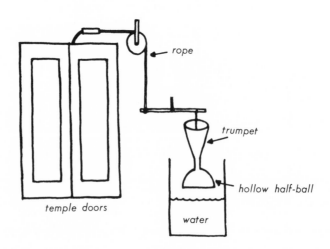

temple doors

rope

trumpet

hollow half-ball

water

# The Mysterious Altar

In Hero's day, the visitor to a pagan temple was at the mercy of its various optical and acoustical contrivances once he crossed the threshold. Bright lights, even pictured images, were projected by burnished metal disks, some shaped like concave mirrors. Echo chambers and whispering galleries produced eerie voices that could be ascribed to any of the countless deities of that pantheistic age. There was even a temple with a rolling floor that was operated by a mechanism in the cellar, to produce the effect of waves or an earthquake.

More substantial marvels were provided for the benefit of doubters, and one of the most convincing was the mysterious altar described by several ancient writers and explained in detail by Hero. It probably originated in Egypt, but was used afterwards in Greek and Roman temples.

The altar was a heavy pedestal, surmounted by the statue of a goddess. Worshippers would kindle a fire on the altar to pay tribute to the goddess. Although it was customary to pour wine upon such a sacrificial fire as a libation to the gods, in this case the worshippers were told to desist. Then, after a breathless wait, the statue itself poured the libation from a vase held in its extended hands.

Among the people of that day this passed for a genuine miracle and a sign of divine favor. Actually the marvel depended upon the ingenious application of a simple physical law. The pedestal under the altar was a hollow airtight compartment, separated from the fire bowl in the altar by a thin partition. Beneath the airtight compartment was a small reservoir filled with wine. A thin pipe ran up from the reservoir through the statue to the vase it held in its hands.

When the fire was kindled on the altar, the air in the compartment below became heated and began to expand. The pressure of the expanding air forced wine from the reservoir up through the hidden pipe to the vase. By the time the fire reached its height, wine would pour from the vase as a libation. When

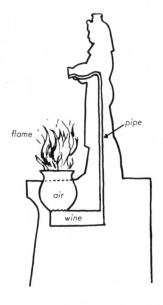

the fire was extinguished, the flow would cease, but the "miracle" would be repeated each time the fire was relighted. The custodians of the temple saw to it that the wine reservoir was always filled and the altar was constantly ready.

# The Ever-Full Fountain

Among the mysteries of the ancient temples were "miraculous vessels" which depended upon hydrostatic laws unknown to the masses. One of the most unusual of these vessels was known as the "Ever-Full Fountain." It consisted of a large bowl filled with water, set on a stone pedestal. The bowl was always filled to the brim; and no matter how much water was dipped from it, the fountain constantly maintained the same level

The secret, as described by Hero, depended on the principle of water seeking its own level. Few people of that era were aware of this

natural law, and those who understood it did not link it to the mysterious fountain. Behind the wall of the temple was a hidden tank, filled with water to the same level as the fountain. A hidden tube ran down from the tank, under the floor, and up through the pedestal to the fountain.

Attached to the side of the hidden tank was a flexible rod with a weight at the outer end and a large wooden disk at the inner. This disk was placed directly under an outlet from a high reservoir, leading down into the tank. When the tank, the fountain, and the pipe

between them were filled with water, the captive disk, floating in the tank, served as a cork. It pressed against the outlet from the reservoir, stopping the flow of water. Thus both the tank and the fountain maintained their proper level. This is shown in the accompanying diagram.

When water was dipped from the fountain, it was replenished from the supply in the tank, running down through the pipe and up into the fountain. The disk fell from the mouth of the outlet, and water from the reservoir flowed into the tank until the disk was raised to stop it.

The working of the fountain was automatic, and it was only necessary to refill the large reservoir whenever it became empty.

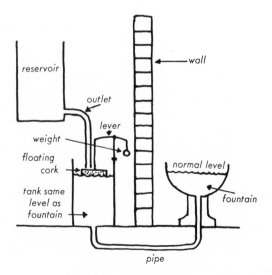

# The Sibylline Temple

opened slowly and mysteriously, as though controlled by some invisible power. Thus the oracle granted an audience to awed visitors who stood outside.

Again, Hero provided the answer to this ingenious device that mystified the public of its day. In fact, he furnished two answers. In each instance, the altar was hollow, with a pipe leading down to the hidden mechanism that actuated the doors. In the more successful version, the heated air was forced into a globe half-filled with water, which in turn was forced through a siphon to an open container suspended by a double rope from a pulley.

As the container gained weight from the added water, it pulled down ropes attached to upright posts. These were extensions of pivots that formed the hinges of the doors above. The ropes, wound around the posts, revolved them to open the doors. When the fire dwindled, the air cooled in the altar and contracted, so that the water was siphoned back into the globe. This reversed the revolution of the posts, and the temple doors closed slowly, majestically—and magically.

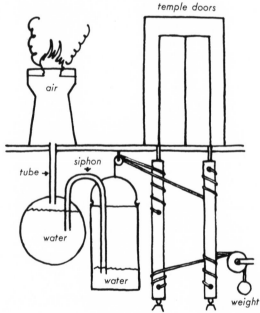

According to Roman legend, when Aeneas went to consult the Sibyl—or prophetess—at Cumae, the doors of the temple opened of their own accord so that the oracle could speak for all to hear. Though the account is mythical, it might have inspired ancient technicians to construct just such a contrivance. Certainly similar devices were included in many pagan temples of a later date.

As with the statue that poured libations, a sacrificial fire was kindled prior to the mystical manifestation. In this case, the altar stood in front of the closed door of an inner sanctum. A little after the fire was lighted, the door

# Hero's Decapitated Horse

Among the many mechanical marvels attributed to Hero of Alexandria, the greatest was the "Decapitated Horse," an automaton that could have its head cut off without losing it. Hero presumably presented this remarkable demonstration at the court of King Ptolemy of Egypt, though it is uncertain to which one of the several rulers of that name who reigned over the land. The magician, whose own exact period is a matter of conjecture, might have lived during the reign of almost any of them.

The miniature horse was made of metal and stood upon an oblong pedestal. First the magician offered it a goblet of wine, which the horse drank. This was a slight marvel in itself. More important, it demonstrated that some sort of internal piping was involved, and that the piping, and the horse, were solid.

So it seemed, at least, until Hero proceeded to perform the real marvel. With a thin-bladed sword, he delivered a cutting stroke down through the horse's neck, deliberately severing its head from its body. Yet, convincing though the blow was, when the sword blade

25

emerged underneath, the horse's head remained exactly as it had been—still firm upon its shoulders!

Nor was this all. As proof that the impossible had been accomplished, spectators were allowed to examine the sword blade. Then the magician offered another full goblet to the metal horse. Amazingly, the automaton drank the wine exactly as it had before.

The inspiration for this feat of wizardry could very well have come from the legends of early Egyptian magic—for the decapitation trick, as performed by Tchatcha-em-ankh and by Deda, was already 3,500 years old in Hero's time. As a leading scientist of his period, Hero was applying his inventive genius toward duplicating the famed feats of an already ancient race.

The mechanism was indeed ingenious. The head and the body of the horse were actually two separate pieces held in place by a series of three wheels. One wheel had three sections, like broad spokes; each of the other two had an open segment, as shown in the diagram. Between head and body was a narrow slot for passage of the sword blade.

In making the stroke, the sword turned the upper wheel, carrying one section from the head into the body, and another from the body into the head. The lower wheels held the head in place during the interim. Upon reaching the first of the two lower wheels, the blade forced its projecting segment downward; and since the wheels were geared together, the projecting segment of the next wheel was brought upward.

This still kept head and body firmly interlocked. And the blade, pressing the projection of the bottom wheel, brought both wheels back to their original position. Thus all three wheels were exactly locked at the start; and all during the operation, at least two were holding the head in place.

The two geared racks which connected the lower wheels slid backward and forward during the operation, carrying a short length of hollow tubing that also cleared the blade when it passed. This tube fitted snugly in the ends of two pipes, which thus became continuous before and after the "decapitation" of the

horse. This pipe led from the horse's mouth through the body and down one leg into a compartment filled with water.

By holding a goblet to the horse's mouth and opening a valve at the bottom of the compartment, a vacuum was created when the water flowed down into a tank beneath. That drew the wine from the goblet through the tube, so the horse appeared to drink. This device was utilized only when the sliding part was in place.

Alongside the horse was the figure of a herdsman. When it was turned away, the horse drank; but when it was twisted about, the horse would stop, as though threatened. This seemed mere byplay, but it served a more important purpose. The figure of the herdsman was connected with a pivot leading down through the water compartment and controlling the valve below.

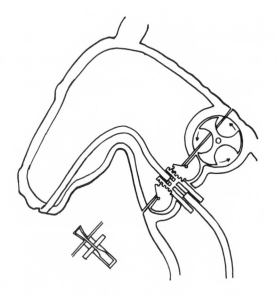

# PART 2

# MAGIC *of the*
# MIDDLE AGES

## Introduction

Belief in the "Black Arts" dominated the Middle Ages, from the decline of the Roman Empire to the rise of modern science. Sorcery, thaumaturgy, and necromancy were the products of the conflict between rising civilizations and primitive beliefs. Fanciful tales of the Arabian Nights genie who responded to Aladdin's magic lamp were matched by legends of Merlin the Magician, who worked his wonders at the court of King Arthur.

In subsequent centuries, popular lore linked science with magic and the supernatural—from Roger Bacon, who predicted many of our modern inventions, through Doctor Faustus, who made a compact with the devil, and paid accordingly. Unquestionably such popular superstition hampered the scientists of that period. Unless they claimed supernatural powers and capitalized upon their peculiar abilities, most scientists were consigned to obscurity and poverty. In any case, they were likely to be accused of sorcery by ignorant neighbors.

Meanwhile, entertainers such as jugglers continued to improve their art. By sleight of hand and other deft displays of skill, they not only awed the populace but amused the nobility. Many of them became court jesters and could pose as necromancers while presenting their tricks in burlesque style, without the risk of being burned at the stake.

Thus, as the trade of the charlatan or pretended miracle worker waned, that of the juggler or trickster increased. By 1584, their methods were so well known that a writer named

Reginald Scot published a book, entitled *The Discoverie of Witchcraft*, which explained many of their tricks. Scot's purpose was to prove that the wonders attributed to wizards and warlocks were either imaginary or exaggerated, since mere mountebanks could imitate them by natural means or trick devices.

Far from improving the situation, Scot's book was promptly banned by King James I, who ordered all copies to be gathered up and burned along with the current crop of condemned witches. Still, some books survived, and in later years new editions appeared. Gradually the spell of witchcraft was broken, though vestiges of it still remain. We can now look back on the Middle Ages as an era when credulity reigned and people generally were deceived by very simple means. Samples of such methods will be found in this chapter.

# Medieval Torture Tricks

Among the wonders explained in Scot's *Discoverie of Witchcraft* were simple tricks of self torture, devices whereby the mountebanks could prove their immunity to harm. These feats were quite effective in the Middle Ages, when people believed implicitly in charms and incantations that would protect them from danger. Imagine the amazement of a group of ignorant peasants witnessing a demonstration like the following: The mountebank showed a pointed implement like an awl or bodkin. Gripping the handle he pressed the point against his forehead and drove it forcibly inward almost to the handle itself. After drawing out the bodkin, he rubbed his forehead repeatedly to stop the flow of blood that kept appearing there. Finally he showed his forehead entirely uninjured and while the audience gasped in amazement he again picked up the bodkin and this time thrust it through his tongue so the point appeared below. Removal of the implement left his tongue uninjured, and the performer finally used the bodkin to bore holes in leather or wood, proving the implement to be quite genuine.

Still more startling was a demonstration given by another member of the troupe, who used a sharp pointed knife much like a dagger. He began by thrusting the dagger straight through his forearm so that the point emerged underneath. He left it there, picked up another knife, and proceeded to cut downward through the bridge of his nose. The spectators expected to see his nose fall off and blood rush from the wound, but neither of those gruesome events took place. Instead, the mountebank drew the blade deftly upward, laid it aside and pointed to his nose, which was intact. He then removed the dagger from his forearm, which also proved to be uninjured. As a finale he took the dagger again and this time drove it straight through his heart, the blade going in clear to the hilt. Yet when he withdrew the dagger he was still unharmed. For a last convincing gesture, the mountebank would pass both the bodkin and the dagger among the spectators, inviting them to test the torture instruments as he had. Naturally, he found no takers.

These tricks depended upon special imple-

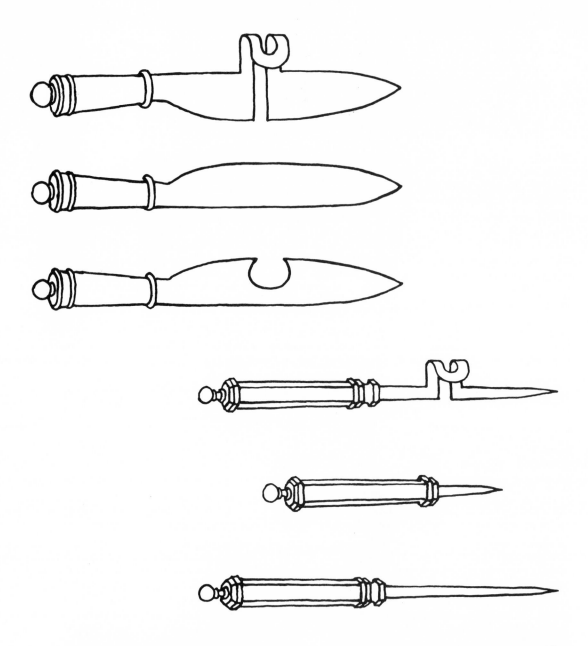

ments which are clearly illustrated in Scot's book of three hundred years ago. The performer used three bodkins: one was quite ordinary; another had a blade which slid into the handle; and the third consisted of two sections with a U-shaped connection. He pretended to pierce his forehead with the bodkin that entered the handle. Upon withdrawing it, he tilted the handle downward so the bodkin dropped to its full length. In wiping his forehead with his other hand he squeezed a sponge that he held concealed there. This sponge was saturated with a red liquid that dripped like blood, and in the course of things the mountebank easily switched the first bodkin for the one with the U-shaped gadget. With a quick move he thrust his tongue into the space and turned his head sideways, holding the connecting portion between his teeth so it could not be seen. Apparently he had driven the bodkin straight through his tongue, but by a reversal of the process he was able to remove it just as readily. During the surprised reaction that followed, he switched this fake bodkin for the ordinary one.

In the dagger trick he again used a two-part blade with a U link when he pretended to drive it through his arm. The removal, as with the bodkin, was simply a reversal. In cutting "half his nose asunder," as Scot described it, he used a knife "having a round hollow gap in the middle"—which meant that a semicircular segment was missing part way along the blade. This was easily covered with an extended finger until the performer pressed the blade upon the bridge of his nose, where the cut-out portion fitted exactly. Later, in removing the knife, his finger again covered the space and the trick was accomplished, except for the substitution of a genuine dagger for the fake one. The dagger driven through the mountebank's heart was another case of a blade sliding into

a hollow handle, but apparently Scot was familiar only with the bodkin, as the daggers in his illustrations have blades too large to fit into their handles. Nevertheless, the same principle applied to the dagger, and if it wasn't used in Scot's day it was introduced soon afterward.

All of these tricks have survived to the present time; and not only were they sold by magic dealers of the early 1900's, they were even included in juvenile magic sets of that period. The one modern improvement is a spring in the handle of both bodkin and dagger, so that the blade automatically goes back into place without tilting the implement downward. In recent years, rubber daggers have supplanted the older style weapon, but their thrust is by no means as convincing as that of the original knife trick.

# The Decapitation Mystery

During the period when jugglers were improving their technique to emerge as full-fledged conjurers, they developed a decapitation trick that was a direct throwback to the earliest mysteries of ancient Egypt. Scot described the trick in 1584 as the "most notable" of "counterfeit executions," so it is probable that this trick was performed long before that time. In effect, a boy was placed upon a table, where he lay face downward, his head covered with a cloth. The magician then reached beneath the cloth with a knife. After performing a cutting operation, he lifted the head within the cloth, showing the boy's headless body. Still covered by the cloth, the head was then carried to the other end of the table and placed upon a platter, the cloth being removed to show the live head on the platter. It was again covered by the cloth, carried back to the boy's neck and affixed there, for when the cloth was removed the boy was fully restored to life.

Two boys were required in this trick, along with a table that had a two-piece top with round holes near each end, resembling a pair

of stocks. The first boy—the only one that the spectators saw—lay face downward on the table while his twin or "double" was concealed beneath. The magician picked up a cloth in which was hidden a head of cabbage, and placed it over the head of the visible boy, who promptly poked his head down into the hole at his end of the table. The wizard carried the cloth to the other end of the table and pretended to set the head upon a platter there. Instead, the second boy simply pushed his head up through the hole in the table and through a corresponding hole in the platter, so that when the cloth was removed the head appeared "on" the platter, still alive. When it was later covered again, the magician again brought the cabbage head into play, shaping the cloth about it while the boy was withdrawing his head downward from the platter. All that remained was the pretence of replacing the head on the neck of the original boy who brought his head up from the hole and was thereby able to rise from the table and take a bow. Originally, spectators may have been conducted into an execution chamber to see the body already decapitated with the head on the platter beside it. According to Scot, the jugglers called it the "decollation of John the Baptist," so it could have developed from one of the Biblical pantomimes presented by strolling players as early as the year 1250. The main difficulty was to keep the viewers from noting the holes in the board when the act was presented in full detail. That meant having the table on an elevated platform so that the spectators could not look down upon the top. Some conjurers may have ended the trick after placing the head upon the platter, letting the viewers decide for themselves whether it was still alive or really dead. Scot himself was rather brief in his account, stating that he omitted many details because they required long descriptions; but he did remind his readers that they should have a tablecloth so long and wide that it almost touches the floor, and

that they should not allow the company to stay too long in the place where the trick was performed.

The decapitation mystery remained popular long after Scot's day and eventually became a feature with many travelling circuses. Instead of a table, an oblong box was used, with a harlequin acting as the executioner and the clown serving as the victim. The holes in the top were neatly fitted trap doors that could not be detected at a reasonable distance. Instead of a cabbage, a dummy head was used exactly resembling that of the clown and his double. The dummy head was kept inside the box and as soon as the first clown's head was covered by the cloth, the double pushed the dummy up through the smooth working trap, so that the magician could lift it under cover of the cloth.

Thus the performer could triumphantly show the severed head while carrying it to the

other end of the box where instead of placing it on the platter he merely set it on the trap door. While the performer was draping the cloth over the dummy head, the double drew it down into the box and thrust up his own head instead. Thus the live head could be shown resting on the box where it carried on a conversation with the performer and, in later times, even smoked a cigarette. Then, when his head was covered, the concealed assistant ducked down into the box and thrust the dummy head up beneath the cloth so it could be carried to the far end of the box, the cloth being lifted to show it during transit. Under cover of the cloth the head was thrust down through the trap door where the double was ready to receive it, and the original performer brought his head up in its place so that he was free to rise and walk away after being restored to life.

# The Wizard's Omelet

Sorcerers of the Middle Ages frequently performed feats of "good" magic to impress and win the favor—and the protection—of the credulous public, particularly when they traveled from their own local community. One of the cleverest stunts of such wonder workers was to concoct something out of nothing, as in the art of "foodless cookery."

A wizard visiting a town would stop at the home of a needy family and offer to reward his humble hosts for their hospitality. His first act was to set a deep pan upon the fire and

to announce that he would prepare a meal for the family by magical means. Drawing cabalistic circles on the floor and reciting incantations, he called upon the good spirits to aid him in the task.

Then he stirred the pan and its imaginary contents with his staff, reciting cabalistic words while the people looked on. Finally his efforts were rewarded: a sizzling noise was heard from the pan. When he lifted it from the fire, there was a large omelet, cooked and ready to eat. The food was given to the family, and the neighbors went away to spread the news that a master of the Black Arts was in their midst—a man who could cook eggs out of nothing!

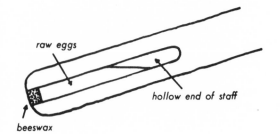

raw eggs

hollow end of staff

beeswax

The secret of the "miracle" was simple, and was effectively employed by many pretenders to magical powers. The wizard's staff was hollow, with an opening at the bottom. Into the cavity thus formed, he poured the contents of a dozen eggs or more. Then he plugged the bottom of the staff with lard, or butter. When the empty pan became warm enough from the fire, the wizard stirred the imaginary food with his staff. This was a perfectly natural action, for his staff was regarded as a symbol of his magical ability, and its use expected. The lard immediately melted, and the eggs poured into the pan where they soon cooked and formed the "miracle" meal that the sorcerer gave to the poor family. With all the humbug and clap-trap that went with this exhibition, the wizard was sure to be successful, provided he did not keep the eggs in the staff for a long time before he used them.

# Cagliostro's Crucibles

Greatest of all delusions that flourished during the Middle Ages was the belief in alchemy, the process whereby base metals could be transmuted into silver or gold. Though the art was attributed to the ancient Egyptians, it was neglected and almost forgotten until after the year 700. About that time Arabian philosophers revived it and began the quest for the "philosopher's stone," an imaginary substance that would make transmutation possible.

The craze spread to Europe and lasted for a thousand years. A long line of alchemists reported various degrees of success and spurred the quest all the more. They were speculating, often stumbling upon discoveries that were to become the foundation of modern chemistry; but at the time, such things seemed miraculous. As a result, alchemists appeared who rigged elaborate laboratories to deceive wealthy dupes.

Their game was to produce enough gold to encourage further and larger investments. They accomplished this through trickery. Then, in the early 1780's, shortly before the French Revolution, there appeared an arch-pretender among alchemists, a man named Joseph Balsamo, who styled himself the Count of Cagliostro, and who ranks among the greatest of all charlatans.

Cagliostro claimed exclusive ownership of two miraculous possessions. One was the "elixir of life," which he said had enabled him to live for centuries. The other was the *materia prima*, a mysterious powder that could transmute base metals into gold. In short, Cagliostro had solved the riddle of the "philosopher's stone," and thereby had become the master alchemist that the world had so long awaited.

When Cagliostro visited Poland in 1780, a private laboratory was prepared for his experiments. There, before a group of skeptical observers, Cagliostro poured a quantity of mercury into a large crucible. To this he added various compounds, including his miraculous powder. The crucible was sealed, placed in a furnace and left there, while Cagliostro and his companions retired to await developments.

After the required period, they returned and opened the crucible. The mercury was found to have changed to pure silver, and Cagliostro achieved fame literally overnight. Having realized the hope of centuries, he was planning further transmutations, when he was suddenly branded as a fraud. A few days after his successful transmutation, a servant, searching a rubbish heap for a lost article, came across a sealed crucible and took it to his master.

When opened, it proved to be the original crucible containing the mercury and other worthless ingredients, including the supposedly precious powder. Obviously, the crucibles had been switched, and in checking back, investigators decided that Cagliostro had used a confederate hidden in the laboratory with a duplicate crucible in readiness. Once the group left the lab, the confederate made the switch, carefully copying the marks on the seals before returning to his hiding place. All very neat, until Cagliostro's helper stupidly tossed the

original crucible on the dump where it was found.

Cagliostro fled Poland in time to escape arrest for fraud, and during the next few years he posed as a physician, offering his elixir of life to wealthy patrons and working fake cures to increase his false reputation. But he dabbled in alchemy on the side and when he arrived in Paris, in 1785, he reverted to his old game with a new twist. In a laboratory of his own, the pretended Count repeatedly performed the experiment of transmuting copper into gold and glass into diamonds. He gave away these valuables, classing them as mere trinkets.

Being familiar with every trick of the trade, Cagliostro resorted to a device used by other pretended alchemists. This was a small crucible with a false bottom made of an amalgam that would melt at a fairly low temperature. A quantity of gold was concealed in the space beneath, and the crucible was shown as an ordinary container. After openly placing copper, compounds, and magic powder in the seemingly simple crucible, Cagliostro would allow it to be covered, sealed and weighed. When the crucible was heated in an open furnace, the false bottom would melt and become part of the worthless dross found in the crucible. When the crucible was opened, small amounts of gold were found amid the residue, proof that the experiment had been partially successful. The fact that the crucible and its contents weighed exactly the same before and after the experiment was a real convincer where skeptics were concerned.

The transmutation of glass to diamonds was simply the same trick, but with diamonds hidden beneath the false bottom. Bits of glass, placed openly in the crucible, were reduced to a molten state by the same intense heat that melted the false bottom. The diamonds, of course, remained unharmed.

According to reliable accounts, all this was but a build-up for more elaborate experiments in which Cagliostro used a furnace of his own, equipped to switch crucibles automatically during the process of a pretended transmutation. But while he was still in Paris, his past caught up with him and he became involved in a court scandal that resulted in his banishment and marked the end of his fame as an alchemist.

# The Demons of The Colosseum

Many self-styled sorcerers of the Middle Ages claimed the power of calling up demons, but few were able to demonstrate that ability on demand. One rare exception was a Sicilian sorcerer whose necromantic marvels were witnessed and recorded in detail by Benvenuto Cellini, the famous Italian goldsmith and sculptor, around the year 1540.

Cellini met the Sicilian while in Rome and found him to be a man of genius, well versed in ancient knowledge. While they were discussing magical arts, Cellini remarked that he would like to see someone invoke demons, and his Sicilian friend calmly offered to produce a horde of them for his special benefit.

The ancient secluded ruins of the Roman Colosseum were chosen as a suitable spot for such a demonstration. So they met there on an appointed evening, each bringing another friend. Within the silence of the vast amphitheater, the necromancer drew circles on the ground and kindled a fire upon which he tossed perfumes and other substances, producing a commingling of smoke and odors.

He then began a lengthy incantation, while there appeared a vast array of devils, which, according to Cellini, completely filled the Colosseum. Apparently, the protective influence of the magical circles allayed any fears felt by Cellini and his friend, for they took the fantastic experience quite calmly.

Arrangements were made for another session in the same setting. This time, they brought along a boy to aid in the ceremonies, which were even more impressive than before. The sorcerer called the demons by name, and they appeared in greater multitudes than the first time. Everyone shook with fear, including the necromancer, while the boy clutched Cellini's hand and pointed out four gigantic demons clad in full armor, who were trying to crash the magic circle.

The necromancer insisted that the demons were only smoke and shadows. Indeed, they gradually diminished in number and faded from view. The party then left the Colosseum and started home, with the necromancer asserting that he had never before conjured up such a ghostly array. But the boy kept pointing out other demons leaping ahead of them, from ground to roofs of houses and back again.

Such was Cellini's story. Some skeptics consider it pure fiction, but it is more probable that Cellini was simply exaggerating an actual experience, which was his custom throughout his autobiography. The logical explanation was that necromancers of the Middle Ages could really produce ghostly images by means of mechanical devices.

These date back to ancient times, when concave metal mirrors were used in pagan temples to project brilliant lights, and even images, upon various surfaces including smoke. One authority, Sir David Brewster, upheld this theory in Cellini's case, even suggesting that perfumes thrown on the fire had a stupefying effect upon the spectators.

That would give too much credit to the pretended Sicilian sorcerer. It is more likely that he used a simple magic lantern—a crude form of the modern projector—to cast still pictures on the towering tiers of the vast and deserted Colosseum. Even better, he might have had half a dozen or so accomplices projecting such pictures from various angles. The smoke from the fire may have caught occasional images, but the mighty background of the Colosseum itself is the only sure solution to the mystifying effect; otherwise, the sorcerer would have chosen some other locale.

The fact that the boy saw demons dancing ahead of the departing group supports the use of the magic lantern. In this instance there was no smoke—nothing but the buildings

themselves. All that the sorcerer's apprentices had to do was race ahead and train fixed projectors on the buildings that Cellini and his friends would pass on the way home.

The magic lantern or optical lantern was first described by Kircher in 1646, a full century after Cellini's encounter with the "de-mons" of the Colosseum. But it is generally conceded that the device was in use long before its closely guarded secret appeared in print. Thus, it might have gone back to Cellini's time, substantiating his story of the Sicilian sorcerer to the last detail.

# The Visions of Nostradamus

Though seers and soothsayers flourished during the Middle Ages, most of them faded into obscurity with the lone exception of Michel de Nostre-Dame, popularly known as Nostradamus. This remarkable but controversial personage actually belongs to the early modern era, but since he followed the traditions of the medieval mystics, he is included in this section.

Nostradamus was born in St. Remy, France, in December 1503. He was a remarkable scholar and once, while studying medicine, he concocted new remedies that stopped the ravages of a plague. He repeated this on later oc-

casions when a pestilence was sweeping the land, and thus gained a reputation both as a physician and a sorcerer, so amazing were his cures.

When rival physicians pressed charges of sorcery against him, Nostradamus retired to his studies; in 1555 he published a volume of poetic prophecies called *Centuries*, which presumably predicted much that was to happen in France and the world at large for hundreds of years to come. Ever since, believers in the so-called "gift of prophecy" have been trying to link great events with the somewhat ambiguous verses penned by Nostradamus. Dur-

ing the four centuries that have already elapsed, some of his "hits" have been surprisingly close, though others have to be classed as highly obscure.

Soon after his book appeared, Nostradamus was summoned to Paris by King Henry II and Queen Catherine de' Medici. The king was somewhat skeptical of Nostradamus' gift, though, curiously, one of the verses closely predicted the circumstances by which Henry was to die a few years later. But the queen, a great believer in astrology, wanted detailed horoscopes of their three sons, Francis, Charles, and Henry.

According to certain accounts, Nostradamus correctly predicted that each would become King of France in turn; and in addition, he created actual visions of the future. These took place in a special apartment, where Nostradamus, a bearded man with an austere air, drew a magic circle on the floor, marked it with cabalistic symbols, and burned pungent powders to invoke the phantasms of the future.

Nostradamus then invited Catherine to gaze into a tilted mirror resting on an ornamental stand beneath a lavish overhanging canopy. To her amazement, the queen saw a throne which was occupied in turn by one son after another, all recognizable despite their varying ages, which were representative of the future. Finally, the throne was occupied by another monarch whom Nostradamus declared would be King of both France and Navarre.

All this took place as the mirror revealed it. Catherine herself lived through the reigns of her sons Francis II, Charles IX, and Henry III, and her daughter Margaret married King Henry of Navarre, who also became King Henry IV of France, following the death of Charles IX. However, some skeptics doubt that Nostradamus made these predictions. They charge that the whole thing was trickery and that Catherine was so amazed that she later fitted events to the scene.

The method, as explained more than a century ago by a French writer on optics, depended on two mirrors. One was in open view on the ornamental stand; the other, set at a reverse angle, was concealed beneath the fringe of the overhanging canopy. When Catherine looked into the visible mirror, it reflected the other mirror, which was tilted toward a secret opening in the wall, leading into an adjoining room.

There, a throne was set up so that impersonators disguised as the three princes could take their proper turns posing as the King of France. Since each was represented at some future age, the matter of make-up was simple, particularly as the distance was too great to allow a close-up of their faces. Nostradamus may have appealed to the queen's maternal pride by introducing the first three impostors as her sons, all future kings, and the fourth as

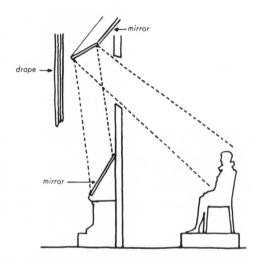

ruler of both France and Navarre, an alliance which he regarded as inevitable.

The device was a prototype of the modern periscope, which was not developed until about two centuries later, so it was not surprising that anyone looking into the magic mirror would accept the reflected images as "visions," just as Queen Catherine did. Either the viewer was drawn away from the mirror between each change; or the mirror was tilted to another angle by a concealed lever from the other room. The queen would then have seen her own face between the visions, making them all the more wonderful.

# Fire Eaters

The power of fire is a mighty force that has awed and terrified man since the beginning of time. Mythology teems with tales of terrible flame-breathing monsters, while hideous fiery idols added a realistic touch to such lore. But it was not until the year 134 B.C. that the human element entered in the person of a Syrian named Eunus, who stirred the slaves of Sicily to revolt against their Roman masters. Eunus established his claim to leadership by exhaling jets of flame as a sample of his supernatural powers.

The Roman consul Publius Rupilius proceeded to smother Eunus, flames and all; but fortunately, the secret of his fire-breathing act was preserved for posterity by the historian Florus. He stated that Eunus used a nut-shell containing sulphur and fire. The shell had openings at both ends, so that by concealing it in his mouth and blowing gently through one end, Eunus projected flames from the other.

Other fire-breathing wonder workers were reported under the reigns of the Roman emperors Hadrian and Constantinus, but it was during the Middle Ages that the art of handling and even eating fire gained great impetus. To carry glowing coals, to hold and even lick white-hot iron, to thrust a bare arm into and out of flames, were typical of the ordeals which were used to determine a person's innocence or guilt regarding certain crimes.

Methods of resisting fire were even published during that period, and with the passing of the ordeals, such secrets were acquired by mountebanks. By the year 1633, there were reports of fire eaters, whose fame as well as their skill grew rapidly during the next two centuries. By then, the art was gradually relegated to dime museums and circus sideshows, but these survivals of medieval magic still awe and impress spectators today.

The fire eater sets up a table covered with

various preparations and paraphernalia. He exhibits a brazier of blazing charcoal; and blandly lifting one of the burning chunks with a fork, he deliberately places it in his mouth and chews it. He ignites a bowl of kerosene, takes up some of the blazing oil with a spoon and transfers the liquid fire to his mouth, apparently swallowing it. He dips molten metal from a cauldron and chews this concoction until it becomes solid, then removes the lump from his mouth. Finally the fire eater holds a flame close to his mouth and his breath breaks out into a huge streak of flame resembling that of a gas-jet, or he can blow a stream of smoke and sparks from his mouth so that he seems to be a human volcano.

There are various principles upon which successful fire eating depends. First and most important is that the mouth, when well filled with saliva, becomes almost fireproof and can withstand much higher temperatures than the hand. Besides this, the fire eater employs many other principles in his feats which the spectators cannot see. He mixes pieces of white pine in with the coals. Charcoal will ordinarily burn the mouth, but white pine will not. The softness of the wood distinguishes it from the other coals and the performer can pick it up easily with a fork. As soon as the blazing wood enters his mouth, he closes his lips tightly and holds his breath. The flame is instantly extinguished. *The fire eater never inhales.*

When he "swallows" burning oil, the performer does not ladle up liquid, but merely lets the spoon become wet. The few drops that adhere will burn for a moment, giving him time to raise the spoon to his mouth. Then he exhales, extinguishing the flame, and immediately takes the spoon in his mouth, as though swallowing the oil. Chewing of molten metals until they become solid is accomplished by using an alloy of bismuth, lead and block tin, which has a very low melting point. It is dropped upon the moist tongue where it will harden without burning and becomes a solid lump.

The volcano and gas-jet feats are very effective when performed in a slightly darkened room and are produced by using certain liquids saturated in cotton. The most practical mixture has naphtha as its principal component. The cotton is secretly introduced into the mouth and the fire eater's breath will ignite when he exhales, but he must always close his lips immediately after, especially when chemicals are introduced into the mouth to add to the volcano effect.

# The Secret of The Burning Oven

Man's inability to withstand heat led to the worship of fire in ancient times, and during the Middle Ages fire was considered an "element" equal in importance to air, water, and earth. Certain men achieved the partial conquest of fire through knowledge of the principles of heat resistance, and the greatest of these "fire kings" was Julian Xavier Chabert, once a soldier under Napoleon, who performed all the feats of his medieval predecessors and revived old wonders that had been long forgotten.

His greatest mystery was called the "Burning Oven," and it brought him to the heights of fame. The oven was really an iron chest within which a fire was kindled until a temperature of 600 degrees Fahrenheit had been registered. The extraordinary Chabert then entered the oven, carrying with him several raw steaks, and closed the door behind him. There he remained, in the fiery furnace, while the spectators looked on in amazement. At intervals his muffled voice could be heard, proving he was still alive; then, after several minutes of suspense, the doors were flung open and out stepped the "fire king," carrying the thoroughly cooked steaks.

As Chabert's fame spread, several people attempted to imitate him and duplicate his

feat; but the secret of his burning oven remained unknown until many years later. It depended on the fact that heat rises, and therefore, when the upper part of the oven becomes extremely hot, the lower part remains cool by comparison. The oven was large, and the fire was kindled in the center. Tests of the heat were taken directly over the fire—not around the lower sides of the oven.

As soon as Chabert entered the oven and closed the doors, he quickly hung the steaks on hooks arranged directly above the fire. He then dropped to the floor by the door and pulled over his head a hood made of heavy cloth, attached to his shirt. In the bottom of the oven were small air-holes through which the performer breathed and thus passed his time until the meat was cooked. Meanwhile, the upper part of the oven grew hotter and hotter, so that when Chabert emerged, a thermometer placed above the fire registered the terrific heat of 600 degrees!

When he was ready to conclude the experiment, the "fire king" slipped back his hood, arose, seized the steaks, flung the doors open wide, and stepped forth triumphant.

# The Invisible Girl

Two centuries ago there appeared in Europe the sensational phenomenon of an "Invisible Girl." This wonderful person first made her appearance, invisibly, in Paris. She was supposed to have been born in a French province, and because of a retiring disposition she was kept in a glass casket, presumably to insure her safety. It was impossible for the human eye to perceive her, yet she could speak and make her presence known.

The casket was suspended by four chains from the ceiling of a room in an old house. The bottom and the ends of the casket were solid, but its top, front, and back were made of glass so that people could see through. From one end of the casket extended a horn, similar to the phonograph horn of the early twentieth

century. Curious visitors spoke their questions into this horn, from which issued the answers in the voice of the invisible girl.

Tremendous interest arose wherever this prodigy was shown, for the mystery could not be explained. That there could be such an invisible girl was incredible, yet there seemed no other logical solution, since the casket was suspended away from the ceiling and walls, and it was not large enough to contain a human being. Many conjectures were made. One theory attributed the wonder to ventriloquism, but this was soon discredited. Another, which gained credence, was that a tiny dwarf was concealed behind the horn in the end of the casket. This hypothesis was also rejected on the basis that if there were such a tiny mortal alive,

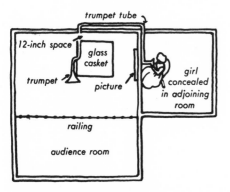

```
trumpet tube
12-inch space    glass
                 casket
trumpet              picture    girl
                                concealed
                                in adjoining
                                room
              railing
          audience room
```

it would have been far more profitable to exhibit the midget than the invisible girl.

The real secret was finally revealed after the mystery had defied all observation and explanation for many years. There was, of course, no "Invisible Girl." Instead there was a real girl who answered the questions from another room. Through the wall behind the casket ran a speaking tube in a line with the far end of the horn, which was built into the frame of the casket.

When the girl spoke through the tube, her voice carried perfectly into the horn. The fact that it was slightly muffled made it sound exactly as though it came from the cabinet itself. People could see a space between the casket and the wall, but it was too narrow to walk through. There was also a picture on the wall, with a peep-hole through which the girl observed objects held in front of the casket, and described them in full detail.

# Catching A Cannon Ball

This spectacular trick originated in the early 1700's as the result of a controversy regarding the velocity of a cannon ball fired from a nine-pounder cannon. A "miracle man" of that day boasted that he could catch the cannon ball at a distance of ten yards, even though the cannon was loaded with a full charge of powder.

The test was arranged, and the gun was loaded in the presence of a crowd of curious witnesses. The miracle man arrived and took his stand; then the cannon was fired by a man who wore a hood, so his identity would not be known in case the experiment failed. When the cannon roared, the human target staggered and reeled back; but as the smoke cleared, he regained his balance and stepped forward uninjured, triumphantly displaying the cannon ball clamped against his chest.

The feat proved so sensational that it was repeated at intervals, always with great success, and it was described in the London *Annual Register* of 1772. After its exhibition that year, it was imitated by other men who had learned the secret; and although there were some serious injuries, the wonder was still performed late in the nineteenth century by Count Petrizio, an Italian magician who caught cannon balls in the center of the bull-ring in Havana and Mexico City. Its secret was virtually unknown except to a chosen few, who carefully guarded it and used it to their own advantage.

The clue to this most amazing exhibition lay in the loading of the cannon, which was done by friends or confederates of the performer prior to his arrival. Although the full charge of powder was used, only a small part of the powder was placed in back of the ball. To load a "muzzle loader" of the type employed, the powder was first poured in the mouth of the cannon and pushed down with wadding, with the aid of a ramrod. Then the ball was inserted. While loading the cannon for the exhibition, however, the clever confederate who held the measured charge of powder saw to it that only part of the powder preceded the cannon ball. Then came the wadding and the ball in quick succession. Finally, the remainder of the powder was inserted with an extra wadding. Thus there was

no trace of any left-over powder: all was used.

The wadding was made soft so it would scatter. When the fuse was lighted, the full charge of powder exploded with the usual noise, but only that powder behind the ball actually functioned. The ball's velocity was by no means slight, but the heavily padded performer was able to stop it within the required range of ten yards.

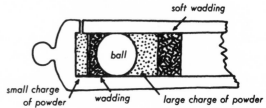

soft wadding

ball

small charge of powder

wadding

large charge of powder

# PART 3

# MODERN MYSTERIES

## Introduction

Today's "miracle man" is the scientist, for the wonders of the modern world have come about through invention and discovery, through scientific research and experimentation. But the triumph of science was slow indeed, and accompanied by many setbacks.

Sailing westard in 1492, Columbus depended upon the scientific marvel of the mariner's compass. But when the compass needle deviated from true north to the magnetic north, his crew was ready to abandon science and return to superstitious belief that the ocean ran downhill into a realm of darkness where the gigantic hand of Satan waited to clutch unwary mariners, ships and all. Fortunately, land was sighted before a mutiny erupted, but superstition still prevailed.

A century later, a Dutchman named Lippershey put two lenses together to form a primitive telescope. When his friends looked through it, they couldn't believe it magnified the object they viewed; instead they thought it brought the weather-vane from a church steeple down to them. Many a new scientific instrument was first considered a magical device.

The explorers who followed Columbus discovered that the peoples of the New World were superstitious, too, and believed in magic; Indian tribes had medicine men and witch doctors who were the counterparts of the European sorcerers. The Aztecs' wise men accepted Cortez and his Spanish soldiers on horseback as living gods. The Iroquois Indians thought there was magic in the "firesticks" of Champlain's musketeers, who mowed them down near the shore of the lake that still bears his name.

Among the explorers themselves, as among the most primitive tribesmen, anything unknown or unfamiliar was a marvel which they attributed to magic. They brought back fanciful exaggerations of the wonders they had seen or heard about in America, such as Florida's "Fountain of Youth," the golden cities of Cibola, and the Patagonian giants. Similarly, every new scientific invention—from lightning rods and balloons to early steam engines—impressed the general public of its day as something magical and mysterious.

But after many years, science came into its own, and it then became the fashion to class anything marvelous as "scientific," whether or not this was true. Soon the methods of science were being openly applied to the development of magical effects, and the new age of marvels was at hand. The examples that follow should have put an end to superstition, but they apparently have not, for even in this modern age of space exploration there are still people who believe in magic.

# Franklin's Miracle

Among the first practitioners of modern scientific magic was Benjamin Franklin, who found that he could excite people's curiosity about comparatively simple experiments by presenting these in a mysterious, magical style. As a youth, he always carried a purse made of asbestos—at that time a rare and little-known substance—so he could demonstrate its immunity to fire whenever he met persons who might be interested. When asked why he used the fireproof material for a purse, young Franklin quipped that it was "to prevent his money from burning a hole in his pocket." This lifelong ability to convey the most marvelous inventions and discoveries with a humorous touch, so characteristic of Franklin's wit, has been copied by successful magical entertainers up to the present day.

One of Franklin's most fabulous near-miracles was performed for a group of intellectuals at the home of Lord Shelburne in England. They were strolling through the adjoining park when they came to a wide stream; Franklin, then sixty-six years of age, stopped, and leaning on his cane, pointed to the wavelets that were lashed by a brisk breeze.

Solemnly, Franklin announced that he could calm the water by his magical powers. While his companions smiled, anticipating some brilliant jest, Franklin walked upstream, raised his cane above the water, and imperiously commanded the waves to cease. To the onlookers' amazement, the stream promptly calmed until not even a single ripple disturbed its surface. Awed by this incredible result, the group returned in silence to Shelburne's mansion.

There Franklin explained his feat. He had read, in the works of the Roman author Pliny, that the sailors of ancient times had poured oil on a turbulent sea to quiet it. Franklin accordingly tried it out on a pond, and he discovered that a mere spoonful of oil, poured on the windward side, would spread and smooth a surprisingly large area of wave-streaked water.

To dramatize his findings, Franklin duplicated, perhaps borrowed, a trick from the Middle Ages—that of the "Wizard's Omelet," where the contents of several eggs were secretly stored in a hollow cane, from which they were later poured into a pan. Franklin's cane was also hollow, being made of bamboo,

and its upper section contained the oil, which could be released by unplugging a tiny air-hole.

Thus, by taking his stance upstream and waving the cane, Franklin sent the spreading oil-slick down toward the surprised spectators, who were so amazed by the quelling of the waves that they failed to notice the slight film that streaked the water's surface.

Franklin worked his cane trick on other oc-casions, but always with the hope of interest-ing his fellow scientists to try the experiment on the larger scale described by Pliny. A year later, they poured oil on a rough sea of Ports-mouth, England, and though the trial was only partly successful, it paved the way to later tests. In modern times, Franklin's "miracle" has been used again and again in aiding rescues at sea.

# The Automatic Chess Player

During the eighteenth century many advances had been made in the creation of automata, or automatic figures. At the height of this progress appeared the famous "Automatic Chess Player," one of the most ingenious and mystifying contrivances ever invented; its career rivalled the fantasies of fiction. The first chess player was built in the year 1769 by Baron Von Kempelen, a Hungarian, and it later became the property of J. N. Maelzel. The player was a life-size figure, seated on top of a box before a chessboard. There were doors in the box and in the figure of the player, all of which could be opened to display masses of intricate mechanism.

With its cold, fixed gaze, the automatic player would seem to read the very thoughts of its human rival; then with a slow, swinging motion of its right arm, the figure deliberately grasped a chess piece and made its move. Hu-

man skill seemed to have no power against this marvelous mechanical device, and the automaton won game after game. Its secret was carefully guarded—because it was not an automaton at all! It was operated by a concealed

**1**

**2**

**3**

assistant who stayed in the box beneath the figure.

The explanatory diagrams show how concealment was made possible. When the large door was opened for inspection, the assistant moved to the left side of the box, in back of the machinery which only occupied a narrow front section. As soon as the door was closed, the concealed person swung to the right side of the box, and pushed the machinery to the left where two small doors were opened. During this time, another door could be opened in the body of the figure. Then all the doors were closed and the hidden player entered the figure and peered through tiny holes in the body. Thus he could see the board and his opponent's moves, and could calculate the plays of the figure. A pincer-like arrangement in the figure's hand enabled the hidden operator to pick up the chess pieces. His position, as he operated the arm and played the game, is illustrated.

The original automatic chess player had an extraordinary history. It played the Empress Maria Theresa of Austria and later, in 1809, defeated Napoleon in the Palace of Schonbrunn, in Austria. The concealed assistant was a man named Allgaier, an expert chess player who enabled the figure to live up to its reputation. According to the story, the automaton had been taken to Russia in 1796 where it was used to aid a Polish officer named Worousky to escape from that country. Worousky had lost his legs in battle, and made an excellent operator on that account. He was a skilled chess player and the figure, it is said, defeated Empress Catherine while he was the hidden operator. When Maelzel obtained the automaton, he used an assistant named Schlumberger, and visited the United States and the West Indies. The figure was later exhibited at the Chinese Museum in Philadelphia where it was destroyed by fire in 1854.

# The Ghost Gun

hollow bullet
containing red dye

In 1856, the French conjurer Robert-Houdin was sent to Algeria on a strange mission. Tribes of Arabs inhabiting the Algerian wilds had rebelled against French rule, and the cause of their revolt had been attributed to the Marabouts, or Algerian magicians, who claimed to receive aid from powerful invisible spirits. The French government decided that if the Arabs could be convinced that a Frenchman possessed greater magic powers than the Marabouts, the tribes would soon cease their warlike preparations. Accordingly, Robert-Houdin went as a special emissary to Algeria to mystify the natives. He was heralded as a sorcerer of uncommon ability, and many Arab chieftains were summoned to witness his exhibitions.

So great was the success of the French magician that he made a short tour among the neighboring tribes and introduced the famous "ghost gun" which ended the fame of the Marabouts. When he came to an Algerian town, he declared he would kill one of the invisible evil spirits of which the Marabouts boasted. This was a bold announcement, for the Marabouts claimed that the spirits were immortal and could not be harmed by a human being.

The French wizard took a rifle, loaded it, and waited near a small building for the invisible enemy whose presence he claimed he could detect. Suddenly he appeared to see something near the wall, although the Arabs saw nothing. Raising his rifle, Houdin fired at the wall, then started forward, announcing that he had wounded his invisible enemy. When the Arabs reached the spot, they were amazed to see blood stains on the wall. The stains were fresh and wet and they were at the very spot where the "ghost" had stood.

The power of the Marabouts was forgotten, while the fame of the French magician was heralded far and wide. Here was a man who could see, wound, and put to flight the demons of the invisible world!

The secret of Houdin's "ghost gun," as he himself revealed it, was quite simple. He used special bullets, hollowed, filled with red liquid, and plugged at the front end. When such a bullet struck the wall, it smashed and the "blood" appeared instantly on the surface of the wall. The witnesses who were close enough actually saw the bullets take effect and "wound" the "ghost"!

# Sword Swallowing

Many witnesses have marveled at the performances of sword-swallowers, exhibitions so baffling as to seem truly incredible. The capable sword-swallower uses a rack of dangerous weapons—large swords, sabres, pointed saws, and other sharp implements. Taking a sword, he bends back his head and slowly pushes the point of the blade into his mouth. Down goes the sword, almost to the hilt. Then it is withdrawn, flourished in the air, and again swallowed almost to its full length! The sword-swallower repeats his feat with other weapons. He continues by partly swallowing two or three swords at one time. A bayonet, attached to a rifle, disappears down the performer's throat. A sword is swallowed to half its length; then the performer places the butt of a rifle against the handle of the sword and discharges the gun. The recoil drives the sword down to the very hilt. Some of the most daring sword-swallowers have used red-hot weapons in their exhibitions.

The onlooker is nonplussed; the performance seems unbelievable.

There must be a trick to it, but where? Stories have been told of swords with loose blades that slip back into the handles, but the sword-swallower devours a blade that is five times as long as the handle. The true, little known secret of sword-swallowing is as amazing as the feat itself, for there is no trick to it. The performer actually swallows the swords.

The explanation lies in the fact that the passages to the stomach, namely the mouth, the pharynx, the esophagus, and the stomach itself, can, by long practice and careful experimentation, be brought into an almost straight line capable of admitting the blade of a sword. The sword-swallower must serve a long apprenticeship, during which he accustoms his mouth and throat to the touch of steel. Then, with each experiment, the blade can be inserted farther and farther down the alimentary canal, until the sword-swallower can manage a sword blade over twenty inches in length.

The swords are usually made in one piece, the blade and the handle cut out of the same piece of metal. This avoids the possibility of the handle breaking from the sword. The performer is very careful in his choice of weapons, making sure to use those which are suited to his requirements. Many sword-swallowers secretly attach hard rubber points to the tips of the swords to prevent injury as the sword is pushed through the passages. Another safety device is the "guiding tube," a sort of sheath which is swallowed by the performer before he appears on stage. Such a sheath is necessary when the rifle is used to drive the blade down the throat, and also when red-hot swords are swallowed.

# The Electric Girl

Long a featured attraction at carnival side-shows and freak museums, the act of the "Electric Girl" has awed generations of baffled spectators. Electra, as she was often called, appeared to be an ordinary young lady, but according to the lecturer who introduced her, she was capable of withstanding huge electrical shocks that would mean death to any other mortal.

Even the dread electric chair had no terrors for Electra, who calmly sat in such a contrivance while the wires were connected and the switch pulled. The lecturer then told the audience that thousands of volts were passing

through the girl's body; and to prove it, he had Electra raise her arm, while he placed a long blue tube against her wrist. Instantly, the tube lighted, while the audience gasped.

As a further test, the operator would dip a piece of cotton into a bottle of gasoline, and extend it on the end of a wire. As it touched the girl's hand, the cotton burst into flame. Members of the audience were allowed to touch the girl's fingers. They immediately received a sharp shock, and sparks leaped from the girl's hand. Other dramatic and convincing tests were used to prove that Electra possessed some uncanny power.

Actually, the act depended on a special transformer in the platform beneath the electric chair. This was used to produce a "high frequency" current that was high in voltage, but low in amperage and therefore lacked destructive power. By pressing her arm against an arm plate in the chair, the girl received the full current, but scarcely felt it. The bulb which lighted on contact with the girl's wrist was a mercury arc, designed for a high frequency current; an ordinary incandescent bulb would not have lighted. Anyone could play the part of Electra and survive the ordeal unharmed.

One self-styled "electrical wizard" of the early 1900's put on an elaborate stage show of this type, once offering to sit in the electric chair at Sing Sing Prison when the full current was thrown on. Luckily for him, his challenge was ignored.

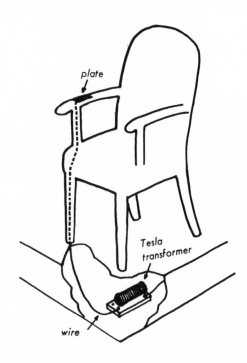

# The Mysterious Ball

Near the close of the nineteenth century, a mystery was presented in Paris that offered no plausible solution and perplexed the keenest observers. A ball little more than two feet in diameter rested on an incline. At the command of the demonstrator, the ball began to move, impelled by an unseen force. It rolled up and down the incline according to the man's instructions, finally descending and rolling off the stage. If this mysterious ball were exhibited today, numerous theories might be propounded: "electro-magnetism," "radio control," or other explanations involving electronics, but the people of that day had no such

theories to consider and were completely mystified.

Despite the small size of the ball, there was a human being inside it. The sphere came apart in two sections, and the operator, who was a wonderful contortionist, fitted himself into one of these. The other half of the ball was then clamped into position. Tiny air-holes allowed the hidden man to breathe. The actual diameter of the ball was thirty inches; beside a man six feet tall, it looked extremely small. It required an expert contortionist to take his place inside the ball, and through long practice he acquired the knack of making it

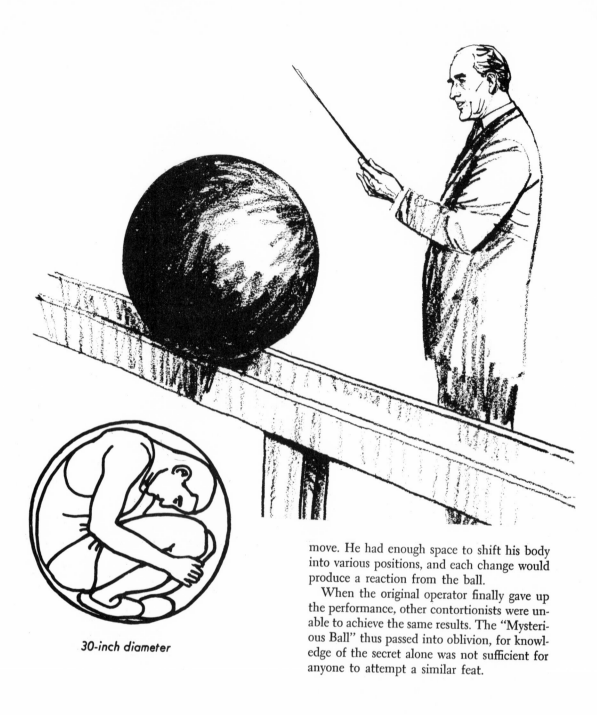

30-inch diameter

move. He had enough space to shift his body into various positions, and each change would produce a reaction from the ball.

When the original operator finally gave up the performance, other contortionists were unable to achieve the same results. The "Mysterious Ball" thus passed into oblivion, for knowledge of the secret alone was not sufficient for anyone to attempt a similar feat.

# The Human Fly

In the years before 1900, European audiences were thrilled and chilled by the sight of a man walking upside-down. This performance took place upon a heavy board suspended near the dome of a theater; at each end of the board was a trapeze. The "Human Fly" was lifted

concave rubber "sucker"

"sucker" attached
to shoe

to a trapeze, on which he swung back and forth until he was able to press his feet upward against the board. Then he let the trapeze swing away while he stood there, upside-down, with no visible support. Taking slow, careful steps, he walked along the board to the other end, where he swung back onto a trapeze and was lowered to safety.

Amazing though it may seem, the mysterious feat was accomplished by the employment of a simple scientific principle. Attached to each of the performer's shoes was a rubber "sucker"—a concave disc of soft rubber. The edges of the disc were moistened and the surface of the board was smooth and highly polished. Every time the foot was pressed against the board, a vacuum was created. The air was forced out of the concave disc, and the edges, adhering tightly to the board, prevented the air from returning when the extra foot pressure was relaxed.

With a well-constructed "sucker," a few inches in diameter, a vacuum was formed capable of supporting nearly two hundred pounds. Thus the performer was fully supported by one foot while he moved the other foot forward. The "suckers" were carefully prepared so that a sharp pressure of the heel would lift the edge of the rubber disc and cause the adhesion to cease. In this manner, one foot could be released when the other had been affixed to the board. From a very short distance, the presence of these rubber discs could not be noticed. The performer usually was a man of comparatively light weight, so that the discs would not be taxed to their capacity.

# The Bullet-Proof Man

Late in the past century there appeared a public performer who claimed to possess a marvelous secret which rendered him immune

to gun-fire. He attributed his invulnerability to an extraordinary new invention which he claimed as his own: he wore a light-weight padded coat which was his sole protection against bullets. On numerous occasions, he offered himself as a target for skilled marksmen, who had the privilege of using their own rifles and cartridges.

Standing with his back to a wall, he was uninjured after several bullets had been fired into his protecting jacket. His successful exhibitions brought him offers of large sums of money for the secret, but he kept his knowledge to himself. However, the career of the "Bullet-Proof Man" came to a most unfortunate ending. During one of his demonstrations, the coat failed to protect him, and he received a wound producing complications that resulted in his death.

Later, when investigators inspected the jacket, the mystery was solved. The surprising truth about the "Bullet-Proof Man" was the fact he had not been killed earlier. Instead of some unknown and mysterious substance in the lining of the coat, the investigators found nothing more than a quantity of powdered glass! Unquestionably this means of protection was effective, since it had proved so on more than one occasion. But his coat was not absolutely bullet-proof. It had simply been a question of time before a bullet found a weak spot in the lining of the coat and delivered the fatal wound.

The simplicity of the device was the chief reason why the man had guarded his secret so carefully. As long as he maintained an aura of mystery, people failed to guess the secret and he had been regarded as a modern marvel. None of the people who discovered the secret cared to use it for themselves. They had expected to find a wonderful contrivance which could be brought to perfection, but they were disappointed. Since then, many bullet-proof jackets have been made and are available, but none of them has created such a sensation as did this wonderful coat with its padding of powdered glass.

# The Georgia Magnet

In the year 1884 there appeared in New York a young woman named Lulu Hurst, who styled herself the "Georgia Magnet" or the "Georgia Wonder." She was the reputed possessor of an invisible power called the "Great Unknown," a strange force which seemed to enter her body and invest her with superhuman strength. While under its influence, she could push several people around a stage,

despite their efforts. If she held a cane in front of her, two men pressing against it were unable to push her from her position.

Another test of this invisible power was performed with a billiard cue. Holding the cue in a vertical position, a man would attempt to push it against the floor, while the "Georgia Magnet" rested the palm of one hand against the cue. His efforts would prove to be of no avail: the invisible magnet power seemed to paralyze him.

The feats demonstrated by Lulu Hurst baffled the keenest observers. It seemed certain that a modern miracle had been achieved, that some supernatural force actually aided the girl. After several years, she retired from the stage with the power of the "Great Unknown" still a mystery, until later investigation solved the riddle. The whole exhibition depended upon *force deflection*, often seen in our ordinary actions, but generally unnoticed. For example, if a man extends his hands at arms' length and tries to raise a window, keeping his arms horizontal, he will exert a great amount of strength with no result. But if he approaches the window as closely as possible, and pulls it straight up, the task becomes an easy one. On the first attempt much of his force is expended in the wrong direction, but on the second, all energy is exerted upward in the right direction. A bullet, travelling at a high rate of speed, may be deflected by striking a thin surface at an angle. A stone rebounds from water when it hits the water at the proper angle. In a similar manner, the force used against the "Georgia Magnet" was deflected into useless effort.

In the picture on the left, the man is trying to push the cut along the line A—A. But the upward pressure exerted by the woman in the direction of B deflects the man's effort, so that it goes toward H. Much of his energy is expended just in keeping the cut down to the level of his shoulders.

In the picture on the right, the woman's hand presses at A and deflects the man's efforts from the direction of B (toward the floor) to the direction of G. Thus he is continually in danger of losing his balance, and his strength is of no avail.

There are many other remarkable tests similar to these, all depending on the principle of force deflection. That is the real secret of the "Great Unknown," the mysterious "power" which aided the "Georgia Magnet" in her amazing performances.

# The Modern Samson

Many of the stunts performed by strong men are faked, although there are performers who give genuine exhibitions. Some performers mix the tricks with the genuine feats and the public does not know the difference. Disregarding the lesser tricks of strong men, the greatest fraud of this type was perpetrated by a strong man in England, and the secret became known because of a most unusual happening.

One of the stock feats of strong men is the lifting of heavy iron dumb-bells which the average person can scarcely move. A strong man can lift great weights, but the trick is not sensational, for an iron dumb-bell that does not look very large may be quite heavy. Intense competition among lifters led to the faking. First, wooden dumb-bells made to look like iron were substituted for the heavy iron ones. But the trick was exposed. Hollow dumb-bells came into use and were weighed on false scales, so that the strong man would appear to be lifting a weight of double size.

Then there appeared upon the scene a superstrong man who claimed to be a veritable Samson. The final feat of his act was the lifting of a dumb-bell supposed to weigh a thousand pounds and so heavy that two men could not carry it. It took two men to wheel it on the stage on a small truck, and even that effort was difficult for them. Then two powerful men were invited on stage from the audience. They took hold of opposite ends of the dumb-bell and tried to lift it, but they could not move it from the truck. Then they stepped aside and let the modern Samson try it. He took a firm hold on the dumb-bell and slowly

raised it from its resting place. Gradually he extended it above his head, then lowered it to the floor, while thunderous applause came from the audience. Again the strong man raised the dumb-bell, and then he set it in the truck. Apparently exhausted by his efforts, he bowed and walked off stage while his assistants wheeled the dumb-bell away.

During one of his shows, two brawny steel workers stepped on the stage when this modern Samson called for volunteers. They braced themselves, determined to raise the dumb-bell, while the strong man smilingly looked on. As the men raised their shoulders, a strange thing happened. Up came the dumb-bell and the truck with it! As they held the dumb-bell on

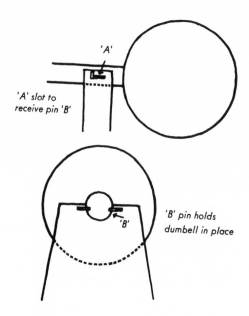

'A'

'A' slot to
receive pin 'B'

'B' pin holds
dumbell in place

'B'

their shoulders, the truck dangled below. The audience was momentarily stunned—then the truth dawned upon everyone.

The dumb-bell was a hollow sham which weighed less than a hundred pounds. It had two slots which fitted into pins in the truck. When the truck was brought on, the dumb-bell was locked tightly in place and could not be lifted. The strong man simply turned it in the right direction, releasing the catches which enabled him to raise the dumb-bell with ease. The truck was so heavy that the average man could only push it, but the combined strength of the powerful steel workers brought the truck up with the dumb-bell.

# PART 4

# MAGIC *of* INDIA

## Introduction

Since Marco Polo wrote of his travels in the Orient in 1300, visitors to the East have brought back fabulous accounts of the wonders they witnessed there. Centuries later, when British domination grew in India, that land became widely known as the home of mystery. By 1900, European and American magicians were touring India, hoping to learn the secrets of remarkable mysteries that they could take home with them to thrill and amaze Western audiences.

To their surprise, they found that the feats of the Hindu fakirs had been grossly exaggerated. In fact, the tricks of the visiting magicians so overwhelmed native audiences that they were invited to make extensive tours through India, and they reaped nice profits. Along the way, they tried to track down some of the fantastic wonder workers who were said to perform their feats in out-of-the-way places like the remote fastnesses of the Himalayas, but to no avail.

Despite this lack of evidence, many intelligent persons remained impressed by the Indian magicians who worked in the open squares of Bombay or Calcutta, while American and European performers required stages and theaters for their acts. In truth, however, each turned his particular surroundings to his own advantage. The Indian conjurer, wearing a long robe and squatting on the ground amid his baskets, had perfected his tricks and deceptions according to the needs of his setting, just as the American magician used his evening clothes, draped tables, and nickel-plated cabinets.

It is not surprising that Indian magic gained its exaggerated reputation. When the British came to India, magic back in England was at a hanky-panky stage. The so-called conjurers were mostly mountebanks who appeared at country fairs with timeworn tricks and trinkets; even if they fooled people with skillful sleight of hand, they lacked the captivating glamour and mystery attributed to the East. Oddly enough, though, the jadoo wallahs, or itinerant Indian magicians used similar tricks, also passed down from one generation to the next.

Indeed, the jadoo wallahs, even to their glib talk, their way of attracting a local crowd and soliciting contributions, were the counterpart of the English mountebanks. But the novelty of their performances made the jadoo wallahs the very personification of magic and mystery for the staid British observer. Soon the simple tricks of these street performers were being identified with the feats of the fakirs, who submitted themselves to incredible tortures and claimed truly uncanny powers.

These, too, were exaggerated; and to strengthen their aura of the supernatural, even more fantastic tales were told of yogis who dwelt in Himalayan caves and communicated with one another by telepathy while floating in midair. However far anyone went to track down the mysteries of India, new and larger mysteries always loomed ahead, like the snow-clad Himalayas themselves.

Meanwhile, in Europe and America, the state of magic had risen to undreamed of heights; stagecraft and science were shattering the myths of mysticism associated with the Far East. But the glamour of Indian magic persists.

# The Colored Sands

According to early accounts, this colorful Indian trick was originally performed with dark sand, light sand, and the reddish dust from bricks. Later, sands of various colors were introduced: green, red, yellow, blue, adding beauty to the fascination of the mystery.

First the magician exhibits and spreads about him a collection of little bowls, each containing sand of a different hue. He then scoops sand from each bowl into a larger bowl filled with water. Modern performers often use a clear glass bowl so the audience can see that no trickery is involved.

Into the water go the colored sands—red, yellow, green, blue—and as the magician stirs them, they form a muddy, darkish brown solution. Then, wiping his hands, the jadoo wallah calls upon the audience to name a color.

Suppose the response is "Blue." He dips his hand down into the murky water, brings up a blob of wet sand, and recites cabalistic words as he squeezes the blob in his fist. Suddenly, dry sand pours from his hand, and it is the very color chosen: blue.

Again he calls for a color, dips his hand into the bowl, and brings it dry from the soggy mess. Red, green, yellow, all pour from the magician's hand in the same wonderful fashion, leaving no doubt regarding the power of Eastern magic.

But there must be a trick to everything that the jadoo wallah does. In this case the trick is quite simple. Beforehand, the magician prepares little wads of colored sand, covers them with grease, and bakes them until they become solid. Each of these wads he places in a small bowl with loose sand of the same color.

When he displays the sands and finally pours them into the big bowl of water, the grease-coated wads go along. The magician keeps close track of their positions while he stirs the water to mix the sands into a muddy mass. He dries his hands, and when the audience calls for a color—such as blue—he makes a quick dip and brings out the coated wad of that particular color. With a squeeze of his fist, the wad becomes loose sand that trickles brightly, completely dry. Since the magician knows the location of the other wads, he proceeds to repeat the process, color by color. Every fistful of dry sand, each another color, adds to the uncanny effect.

American magicians have improved this trick by using sand in water-tight packets that are broken open when squeezed. One performer, Dr. Harlan Tarbell, made a beautiful spectacle of it with a spotlight to heighten the luster of the sparkling sands, turning a comparatively simple trick into a superb mystery.

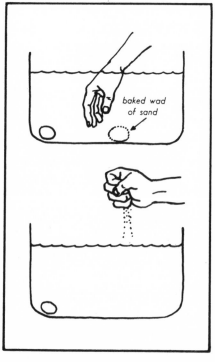

baked wad of sand

# The Jumping Stone

One of the first American magicians to witness the colored sand trick was Samri S. Baldwin, who viewed a primitive yet effective performance in Cawnpore. However, he was even more impressed by the mystery which followed immediately upon it—the riddle of the "Jumping Stone."

Using the same bowl of murky water, the magician showed his audience a small stone shaped like a bird's egg, which he then slowly and deliberately placed in the water. Next he began to pipe away upon a little flute, intently watching the bowl of water. Finally he extended his hand, gave a quick cry, and all at once the stone egg jumped from the water into his hand.

Immediately, the magician passed the stone among the spectators for examination, then turned the bowl on its side and poured out all the water to show that it concealed no elaborate contrivance. Baldwin had been baffled by the trick, but the Hindu wizard parted with his secret for a few rupees, so it was recorded for posterity.

The trick depended on the use of a small metal spring, shaped like a ring, but cut so that one end could be pressed over the other. The lower end was held in place with a small lump of sugar, which was solid enough to resist the constant pressure from the spring. It took only a simple bit of "palming" for the magician to secretly slip this device into the bowl of water at the conclusion of the sand trick. The murky water hid the metal spring completely.

After showing the egg-shaped stone, the magician placed it in the bowl, carefully setting it on the upper end of the hidden spring. While he played away on the flute, he estimated the time required for the sugar to dissolve and kept watching for a slight stir in the water, a sign that the spring was about to snap. He then extended his hand and added a coaxing gesture with his fingers if more time was needed. Either way, the stone seemed to jump at the magician's command.

When he poured out the water, it was a simple matter for the performer to catch the little spring as it came along and palm it in his accustomed fashion, leaving the onlookers to stare at an empty bowl.

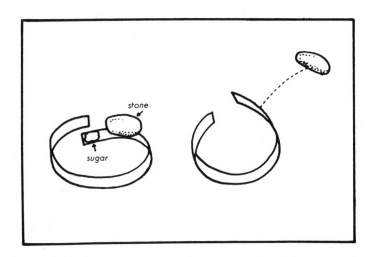

# Indian Snake Charmers

Snake charmers constitute a special group among the "miracle men" of India, with many tricks of their own. Thus they are frequently associated with the jadoo wallahs, who profit from their reputation for accomplishing the miraculous.

Like the jadoo wallah, the snake charmer performs his feats in the open. Moreover, in order to "charm" the deadly cobra, he pipes away on a flute or gourd, using the mystical significance of such music to establish proof of his magic "powers" over the snake.

The snake charmer often begins his act by playing on the flute and causing a hooded cobra to rear up and dance to the music, swaying back and forth with every beat. Members of his troupe may release more snakes from bags and baskets, until several are dancing to the charmer's tune—a startling sight to spectators who fear the death that lurks beneath the cobras' hoods.

When he ceases piping, the snake charmer can make a cobra poise stock-still; at his command, the snake will strike at a tree branch or some other object that the charmer holds, while ignoring the charmer himself. As he handles the deadly reptiles, the charmer lets them crawl over his arms, yet they will strike with violent rapidity at objects held by members of the troupe.

Sometimes the snake charmer will place snakes on the branches of a small tree, then lure them from that vantage point until they are swarming over him as harmless as kittens. Yet no matter how vicious a cobra may become, the skilled charmer always concludes his act by capturing it and calming it as he puts the snake away in a bag or basket.

Much of the effect is simply clever acting on the part of the snake charmer, plus his knowledge of the ways and wiles of cobras. In some instances the snakes are drugged, or have had their venom removed, but even the most deadly reptiles can be handled by a skilled performer. From the start, the charmer deceives his audience by playing on his flute. While snakes have hearing organs and may sense vibrations, they are by no means as susceptible to music as the onlookers suppose. Rather, the dancing cobra merely follows the motions of the charmer, who himself sways to the music. According to one authority, the charmer can make the snake dance without playing on the pipe at all.

Once the movement ceases, the snake pauses, too. It is then ready to strike, but usually waits for its target to come within striking range. If, instead of resuming the dance, the charmer extends a tree branch toward the cobra, the snake will strike at the branch because it represents the immediate threat. To the breathless spectators, this feat seems further evidence of the charmer's uncanny power.

As he handles the cobras, the charmer soon can induce them to crawl over his arms and shoulders by avoiding sudden actions that would excite them. They feel as safe there as they feel on the boughs of trees. Once the charmer has gathered a few snakes in this position, he signals a confederate, who waves some object to attract their attention and excite them. The snakes respond by striking viciously at the confederate, who stays just out of range, but they ignore the charmer entirely.

Similarly, if the snakes are placed on tree limbs, the skilled charmer approaches so slowly that they remain undisturbed. He then stands perfectly still, as though exerting mental control over the cobras. Here again, a confederate plays a secret part in the proceedings. He makes a short but rapid motion toward the snakes to alarm them, but does not come close enough for them to strike. Instead, they desert the tree limbs for the most convenient refuge, which happens to be the charmer,

standing with outstretched arms, posing as another tree.

To conclude his act, the charmer may purposely irritate a cobra by making quick actions with one hand. As the snake begins to strike, the charmer comes up swiftly with his other hand and grips the snake behind the head. He then takes advantage of the cobra's natural urge to hide to put the snake into a bag, thus gaining more credit for his supposedly magical mastery over reptiles.

# The Obedient Cobra

Unlike the jadoo wallah, who depended entirely upon the donations of people who watched his street-corner show, the Indian snake charmer long ago found more lucrative ways to pursue his profession. After convincing people that his power over cobras was truly hypnotic, he would offer to enter bungalows and charm poisonous snakes from their lairs at a rupee apiece and more, according to what the market would bear.

The techniques of these charmers varied. One might squat beside a building and play his flute to coax a cobra from beneath the foundations. Another might prowl about the premises until he found a spot where he felt sure a snake was lurking. Whatever his method, the climax was usually the same, according to reliable reports. With a sudden shout of "Cobra, hai!" the charmer would spring forward and snatch up a wriggling cobra before it could get away. Having bagged that prize, he would go after more, claiming that where there was one cobra, he usually could find several.

Invariably, the charmer could find several, for the snakes were his own. They were hidden in small bags beneath the snake charmer's robe or simply under a waist cloth. Such bags are equipped with draw strings, so that the snakes can be released instantly, and the fakir, being in complete control, comes up with each snake as though he just captured it. Here the snake charmer has an advantage over other tricksters, for the spectators keep a respectful distance; therefore they cannot watch him too closely.

As a result, many snake charmers have traveled all over India, capturing the same cobras time after time and receiving suitable rewards from grateful bungalow owners. However, they may often catch wild cobras, too, for these can be spotted by fresh tracks in the dust or grass. Any such captures naturally boost the charmer's reputation, but perhaps the most impressive feat on record was that of the "Obedient Cobra."

The charmer came upon a snake that was sunning itself on open ground. Instead of driving it away, he motioned other persons back, then slowly approached the snake and assumed a statuesque pose, with his eyes fixed on the snake as though hypnotizing it. Grad-ually, the cobra approached the charmer; and as the man moved backward, it continued to follow him, stopping or going forward at his slightest gesture. Finally, it came so close that he was able to capture it with one deft swoop.

Again, the charmer's knowledge of snakes gave him an advantage over the onlookers. As he approached the snake, the charmer purposely came between it and the sun, so that his robed figure cast a long shadow toward the cobra. Knowing that snakes are near-sighted, he paused far enough away so the cobra was not frightened; but it did see the almost motionless shadow ahead, and took that to be the shade from a tree. So the snake approached the shade, and the charmer drew back. With the shadow gone, the snake stopped, but it moved forward as soon as the charmer artfully put his shadow into range again.

As the inviting shadow receded, the cobra became bolder and followed the charmer in his gradual retreat, finally reaching him when he purposely went motionless. Then the charmer was ready, and made his capture with a flourish. The astonished spectators regarded hypnotism as the only explanation, never suspecting that the shadow was the key to the trick.

# The Marvelous Mango Tree

Outstanding among the fabulous feats of Indian magic is the marvelous "Mango Tree," which, according to many reports, grows from a mere sprout to the height of a dozen feet before the onlookers' very eyes. How this trick gained its fantastic reputation is amazing in itself, yet there are answers to that riddle, too.

The many intriguing and impressive tricks of the jadoo wallah build up to that of the mango tree as the conclusion of his act, and its remarkable effect of mystery is magnified by its climactic position. Often it is performed by a troupe which may include snake charmers, jugglers, and acrobats, all contributing to the excitement of this grand finale.

The magician sets up three poles to form a tripod from two to three feet in height. In the center he places a wide pot filled with soil, or forms a small mound of earth from the ground. There he plants a mango seed about the size of a man's fist, and squatting beside the tripod, he spreads a cloth about it to make a small tent or tepee.

After playing briefly on a flute, the magician removes the cloth and the spectators are surprised to see a small sprout in the center of the mound or pot. Then the tent is formed again and once more the magician pipes away; this time, when he lifts the cloth, the sprout has grown to a foot in height. The whole process is repeated, music and all, and when the cloth is withdrawn for the last time, there is revealed a fully developed mango tree, two or three feet high, its mangoes ready to be plucked and handed to the spectators.

This seems considerably smaller than the exaggerated descriptions of a twelve-foot tree; however, one important point should be noted. None of these fabulous accounts ever mentions the tripod; they talk only about the mango tree. But once the tripod is set up and the tent formed around it, the dimensions of the tent represent the limit to which the mango tree can grow. Using this knowledge as their gauge, trained observers are able to prevent their imaginations from turning fact into fancy.

The "tree" is simply a branch of a mango tree, perhaps three feet in length and bearing a few ripe mangoes. In addition, the magician has two twigs, one quite small and the other of medium size. With the branch, these are hidden beneath large pieces of cloth lying inconspicuously beside the tripod.

When he forms the tent for the first time, the magician brings the tiny twig along with the cloth and plants it in the earth. Then, after playing the flute, he unveils the little sprout. When he next forms the tent, he brings along the larger twig; under cover of the cloth, he sets this in the earth, pipes away, and draws aside the cloth to show how the "tree" has "grown."

By now the audience is watching the pot intently, and the magician takes advantage of this excitement to draw the full-sized branch from under its cloth and introduce it beneath the tent in the same manner. For the grand finish, he unveils the upright branch, which with its ripe mangoes passes for an actual tree.

Explained in these terms, the amazing "Mango Tree" seems somewhat less than miraculous. But to persons unacquainted with the method, it has all the psychological elements of a real mystery, for in their expectancy, eager observers mentally fill in the interludes and imagine that they saw the tree grow during the periods when it was hidden by the tent. Forgetting the cloth and the tripod, all they can recall are the stages of growth: the planting of the seed, its sprouting, the gradual increase in size, and finally the fully developed tree, which they later associate with larger mango trees seen during their sojourn in India.

When he works with a troupe, the magician can perform the trick of the mango tree to perfection, for his assistants help to arrange the cloths with their concealed loads as well as to distract the attention of the audience when the changes are made. And the more skilled performer uses other devices to heighten the magical effect of his act. He may plant a hollow mango seed which contains a hidden sprout; thus he can pull the shoot from the seed very quickly, speeding the initial phase of the trick.

To produce an even larger tree, the magician may use a pliable branch that can be bent in half and secured with cord, so that it originally occupies comparatively little space. He then hides it in the cloth and introduces it in the usual fashion to represent the tree. But in setting this folded branch in place beneath the cloth, the magician releases the cord and the branch springs to twice its size. This permits the use of a larger tripod, or the "tree" may actually emerge above it when the cloth is removed.

1

2

3

# The Indian Basket Trick

The "Basket Trick" is one of the most mystifying illusions of Indian magic. People who have witnessed it in India often describe this feat in terms so fantastic that it seems truly miraculous, but it has been performed abroad by Indian magicians and reproduced by American performers as effectively as in its original setting. When the trick is shown outdoors, with the spectators all around, its magical quality is even more astounding than when it is shown on a stage. Yet the basic method is the same in both instances.

The fakir uses an oval or circular basket, of woven material, having a small round opening at the top. A boy steps into the basket and sits there, hardly up to his hips, with his body and head projecting upward, so that he appears far too big to fit inside the basket. That rather annoys the fakir, who throws a cloth over the boy and keeps trying to press him down beneath it, at first with no result.

Then, suddenly, the shape of the boy collapses, giving the impression that he has disappeared. To prove that the boy is really gone, the fakir jumps into the basket and tramples the cloth with his feet. As if that were not

enough, the fakir himself then squats in the basket, completely filling the space that was hardly large enough to accommodate the boy.

Unquestionably, the boy seems to have vanished. But the fakir does not let it go at that. He furnishes more proof of a most startling sort. He climbs from the basket, removes the cloth, and places a lid over the opening. Then, taking a long sword, he thrusts it completely through the basket, first in one direction, then another, while the onlookers gasp in horrified awe. They can only hope that the boy is gone, for otherwise he would be impaled by the many sword thrusts.

Next, the fakir spreads the six-foot cloth over the entire basket and lifts the cover beneath it, dropping it back in place. He tries this a few times, and suddenly the cover does not drop. It remains fixed, then moves jerkily upward, and when the fakir draws away the cloth, there is the boy standing beneath the upraised cover of the basket, holding it with his hands. He has returned to the basket and emerged unharmed!

From this unexaggerated description of the basket trick, it is easy to understand why some people regard it as genuine magic. Yet it is a wonderful illusion, based on a clever principle which is almost impossible to detect. The chief secret is the deceptive appearance of the basket. It does not seem large enough to contain the boy, but its bulging sides and oval shape provide ample room inside.

As soon as he is covered with the cloth, the boy squirms down into the basket and curls himself around the sides. A basket less than four feet in diameter will have a circumference of approximately twelve feet, so the boy, in his curled position, leaves plenty of space in the center of the basket and toward one side as well. That enables the fakir to trample down the cloth and sit in the basket himself.

The sword thrusts are carefully rehearsed beforehand, so that the fakir misses the boy's body, sliding the blade behind him, between his legs, between his arms and body, and alongside his neck. This convinces the spectators that the boy has really vanished, and since the trick is performed on solid ground, where no trap doors are possible, the disappearance seems miraculous indeed.

While the fakir is covering the basket with the cloth, the boy uncoils, and he comes upright in the center of the basket when the lid is lifted beneath the cloth. The final removal of the cloth reveals the boy intact and the mystery is complete.

In some versions of this trick, the boy reappears from the crowd, or from the branches of a nearby tree instead of from the basket. That can be done quite simply by using twin boys. The one who disappears from the basket remains there until after the crowd has gone, while his brother emerges from hiding at the fakir's signal, thus accounting for the "reappearance."

With a fairly large basket, two persons can be made to vanish, as there is room for both to curl around the sides. Several American magicians have presented the trick in that double form.

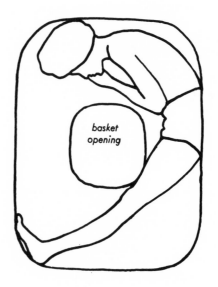

basket opening

# The Hypnotized Weight

The holy men and fanatics of India are noted for their ability to withstand pain, many of them undergoing long and strenuous ordeals of self-inflicted torture. There are human inch-worms, who crawl all the way to the sacred city of Benares, and human logs who roll themselves around the temples after they arrive there. Others hold their hands upward until their arms wither; and one of these Sadhus balanced himself upon a rope and reclined there, day and night, for years. Some brand themselves with red-hot irons, or allow themselves to be hung suspended by hooks, while others have stared at the sun until they have gone blind. Futile though these feats may be, they have awed the populace, and the holy men are regarded as almost supernatural beings. Fakirs and other wonder workers often imitate or adapt such modes of self-torture to their own performances.

Such is the case of the "Hypnotized Weight," which was described in November, 1907, in the *Conjurers' Magazine*, edited by Houdini. The trick was attributed to a magician from Ceylon, and the weight consisted of a small boy tied in a net. First the fakir stared at the audience with wide, bulging eyes, in the manner of a real fanatic. Then he stooped forward and fixed his wild gaze upon the boy.

As the fakir lifted his head, bending backward, the boy rose to the level of the fakir's knees, net and all. Momentarily the hypnotic power of the fakir held him there; then, boy and net descended to the ground.

The explanation is almost as incredible as the feat itself. The fakir's bulging "eyes" were actually thin metal cups that fitted beneath his eyelids and were painted to resemble eyes. Attached to these were strong cords of silk twine with hooks at the lower ends. At the start of the trick, these hooks were attached to the knees of the fakir's baggy trousers.

When he stooped down, the fakir secretly transferred the hooks to the corners of the net containing the boy, meanwhile pretending to hypnotize the boy with his gaze. Then, slowly lifting his head, he closed his eyelids tightly over the cups and drew the boy upward.

By bending his body backward, he brought the cords across his chest, taking some of the strain from the eyelids. After a brief but impressive pause—with the boy in the net suspended in mid-air—the fakir bent forward again and lowered his burden, detaching the hooks after the net reached the ground.

Amazing as it was, the trick had two bad features: it could not be shown at close range, or the cords would be seen; and the fakir's bent back also gave away the fact that some lifting device was being used. So when the Indian fakirs copied this trick, they presented it as a miraculous feat in its own right. Instead of the false painted eyes, they used ordinary metal cups with attached wires leading to a weight. This usually consisted of a heavy stone.

The fakir announced that he would "lift a stone with his eyes" and openly worked his eyelids over the rounded cups. When the fakir raised his head, bringing the huge stone with it, the spectators couldn't believe their own eyes. It seemed as if the fakir was using some magnetic force, perhaps with the wire serving as a conductor. Though only a few bold fakirs presented the trick, its fame spread, and shortly before World War I it was brought to Europe by a troupe of Indian magicians.

There it was witnessed by the English conjurer Austin Temple, who described it in the *Magazine of Magic* for March, 1916, with the following explanation:

"The top eyelid is lifted and a half of the cup is gently slipped under it, and then the bottom eyelid is pulled down and replaced in

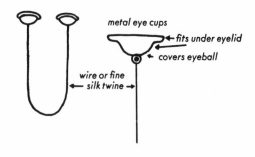

metal eye cups
← fits under eyelid
← covers eyeball
wire or fine
← silk twine →

position to cover the lower half of the cup. The cups are thus brought directly onto the eyelids with the eyelids closed over them, the wires passing out between the lids. The stone is then hung on the wire loop, which covers the two eyecups, and is thus lifted from the ground.

"To prevent the cups from pulling out, the eyelids are tightly closed. It is like a straight, dead pull on a button through a buttonhole, for unless the button is eased through head first, and the cloth eased around it, no amount of pulling will pull it through."

Variations of this trick continued to be performed in India. An English army officer witnessed it near Bombay twelve years later and sent an account of the feat to Ripley, the famous cartoonist, who illustrated it in his "Believe It or Not." The weight in this case consisted of a bag containing a large snake.

# The Human Chimney

A most convincing and spectacular torture trick performed by Indian fakirs is the lighting of a fire on a boy's head. The fakir exhibits a large clay cylinder with both ends open; this he places on the boy's head to serve as a fire box, and into it he stuffs paper, rags, bits of wood, and even pours oil on top. Then the fakir sets fire to the contents of the cylinder,

still adding fuel as the flames spurt upward with increasing fury from the boy's head.

Yet the boy remains unperturbed, apparently immune to the scorching heat. This is attributed to the fakir's magical powers. And when the fire has subsided, the fakir dumps the ashes from the cylinder and shows it empty as before. The boy's head is quite unharmed, and the fakir pats it and sends him happily on his way.

Not only is it a trick, it is a very simple one, which is true of many good tricks. In packing fuel into the cylinder, the fakir intro-duces a flat disk of thick clay. The interior of the cylinder tapers slightly inward, and the fakir takes care that the smaller end is placed upon the boy's head. As a result, the disk becomes wedged as it slides downward, as it

is just a trifle larger than the smaller end of the cylinder.

This confines the fire to the upper portion of the cylinder, with an air space between the clay partition and the boy's head. With the disk properly wedged, the boy scarcely notices the heat as the fire constantly burns upward. At the finish, the fakir removes the cylinder, turns it over and dumps out the clay disk with the ashes and no one is any wiser.

Occasionally, a fakir cooks a meal above the blazing chimney while it is still on the boy's head, making the effect all the more remarkable.

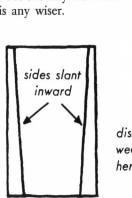

sides slant inward

disk wedges here

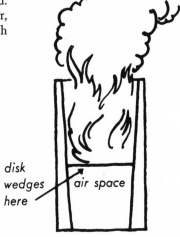

air space

# The Entranced Fakir

For centuries, Indian fakirs and mystics have been credited with the power to float in mid-air. However, it was not until the late 1820's that self-levitation of this sort was actually reported in Madras. An old Brahmin rested one hand on a cane set in a small stool, and remained seated, yogi fashion, four feet above the ground.

Assistants held a blanket in front of the fakir before and after the levitation so that no one could see how he worked the trick. He died in 1830, but his secret did not die with him, for a few years later, a fakir named Sheshal, called the "Brahmin of the Air," performed the same marvel by placing one hand on a rod extending horizontally from the upright cane, while he squatted in the air.

The miracle was seldom seen again until 1866, when Louis Jacolliot, Chief Justice of Chandenagur, visited Benares and met the fakir Covindisamy, regarded as the greatest in India. Along with other mysteries, Covindisamy performed the cane levitation, baffling Jacolliot so thoroughly that many persons doubted the accuracy of his report.

But six years later, the Swedish magician Baron Hartwig Seeman toured India and met Covindisamy, who showed him many of the tricks described by Jacolliot, including levitation. Seeman, however, was more impressed by some of Covindisamy's other mysteries, for by that time European magicians had developed an "aerial suspension" more remarkable than the Indian version.

Still, in the years that followed, the legend of the "Entranced Fakir" continued to grow. Other magicians toured India, hoping to unearth some miracle in the far-off reaches of the Himalayas, but without success. And when they returned home, like Baron Seeman, they developed their own levitation tricks, claiming that these came from India, which only added to the false fame of the ascetic fakirs.

In the late 1930's, more than a century after the old Brahmin had first shown the cane trick in Madras, an Indian fakir brought the miraculous levitation trick to London and performed it outdoors for English audiences and photographers. The pictures, published in many magazines, indicated what had been suspected all along.

The upright cane was really a metal rod,

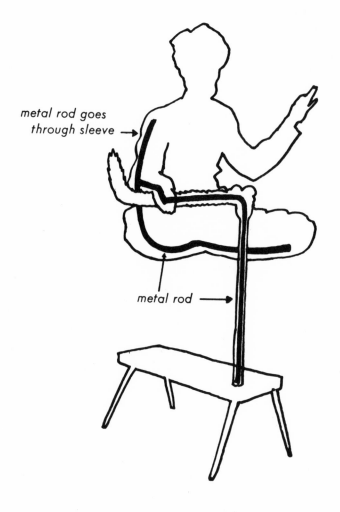

metal rod goes
through sleeve →

← metal rod

disguised as bamboo, fitted firmly in the platform. From it extended a horizontal metal rod, connecting with a curved bar that was concealed within the fakir's flowing sleeve. This continued along his arm and down his back, terminating in a circular seat which supported the fakir in his aerial squat.

Yet despite the obvious trickery involved, many people still believe that Hindu yogis possess the power of levitation. Stories are told of adepts who cross ravines by striding boldly through the air. Others are said to sit in Himalayan caves and gradually float upward through the aid of breathing exercises that render their bodies weightless.

Skeptics have an answer for persons who claim to have undergone such an experience. They say that after sitting cross-legged for several hours, a person's legs become so numb that he feels as if he is floating in air; and if he encourages such a trance-like state, his imagination will carry him to far-off realms. This may be good enough for those who dwell in the Himalayas, but in Madras, Benares, or London, even a yogi needs a metal cane and a curved extension seat to levitate.

# The Indian Rope Trick

Unquestionably the greatest of all the fabled marvels of India is the famous "Rope Trick." This is an open-air performance, and though seldom seen, may be described as follows: A fakir exhibits a long rope and tosses one end into the air. The rope rises high above the upturned faces of the crowd, and a boy climbs the rope to the very top. Then, at the fakir's command, the boy suddenly disappears and the rope falls to the ground.

Such a feat would be worth the rewards of $5,000 to $25,000 that have been offered to anyone who can produce the "Rope Trick" in its full-fledged form, with spectators all around. But though many persons claim to have seen the "Rope Trick," efforts to track it down have proved fruitless. Meanwhile, accounts of the near-miracle have become ever more fanciful and incredible.

According to some descriptions, the rope rises so high that the boy goes out of sight when he climbs it. Then the fakir climbs the rope, too, and also disappears. In other versions, the fakir carries a big knife with him when he vanishes, and then portions of the boy's body come tumbling to earth from the void above. The fakir then reappears at the top of the rope, descends, assembles the boy's dismembered body on the ground and restores him to life.

Hypnotism is the stock answer given to explain such stories. Supporters of this theory claim that only the greatest fakirs can perform the "Rope Trick" because they alone can achieve the remarkable effect, by clouding men's minds to convince them that they had witnessed the wonders described. That is why the "Rope Trick" is so seldom seen: even a fakir possessing the necessary hypnotic power must have a suitable audience under ideal conditions to produce the illusion.

The case is often cited of a photographer who took a picture while the "Rope Trick" was in progress. Later, when he developed the plate, he was amazed to see the rope still coiled on the ground and the boy standing beside the fakir. Presumably the fakir had told the spectators that he was tossing the rope in the air and that the boy was climbing it. The completely hypnotized spectators believed this, although nothing really happened.

The story is filled with absurdities. Mass hypnotism of this sort is practically impossible and beyond the power of any man, especially in such exact detail. Furthermore, assuming that the fakir did hypnotize the entire group, the photographer could not have taken his picture under hypnosis. Or if he managed to take it, he would have focussed his camera on the top end of the rope, where he thought the boy was, and not at the ground. Moreover, if a fakir could hypnotize an entire audience, why should he always limit his performance to the "Rope Trick" illusion when he might make such a captive group believe almost anything?

On the other hand, many investigators insist that the "Rope Trick" is a myth, that it has never been seen in India, and that most Hindu magicians never heard of it until tourists began asking them to perform it. Skeptics attribute the source of the fabled trick to an illustration in an old German book of 1684; this showed Oriental jugglers balancing on bamboo poles and climbing ropes, but the artist's conception was so exaggerated that the people appeared to be vanishing piecemeal into the low-hanging clouds.

Others claim that this myth was publicized after the Sepoy Rebellion of 1857 to encourage enlistment in the British Army, because of the wonderful feats of Indian magic that new recruits would see there. No posters showing the "Rope Trick" are available as evidence, but it

is significant that practically all reports of the trick as now known, have cropped up since that time.

Restrained descriptions offer more plausible clues to the secret of the "Rope Trick." One account estimated the length of the rope as 15 to 25 feet, adding that when it was tossed into the air, it remained there stiff and upright, like a pole. It is possible that imaginative persons, having watched Indian acrobats perform a pole balancing act, have confused this with the "Rope Trick." There are pictures, too, of a boy climbing a short rope, which under microscopic examination appears to be jointed. A hollow rope with articulated sections would be strong enough for a light person to climb when it was rigid, and could be collapsed later by releasing an interior cord.

But there is a better explanation of the "Rope Trick" which accounts for its fantastic reputation yet comes within the mechanical limitations of a fakir's apparatus. The following is perhaps the most plausible version advanced so far: The magician uses a special rope with a hook fixed in one end; the hook has several prongs, bent downward and outward. Until the fakir is ready to perform the trick, he keeps the hooked end of the rope hidden in the coil. The other essential factor in this method is a thin strong wire, stretched from a tree to a building wall or another convenient upright structure some twenty feet above the fakir's head.

Shortly before sunset, the fakir sets up his equipment in the corner of the compound where his wire has been strung. He places the spectators so they face the bright sunlight and cannot see the wire in its glare. After a few preliminaries, he goes into the "Rope Trick," tossing the hooked end of the rope at an upward angle so that it strikes the wire. As the rope slides downward, one of the prongs catches the wire and the rope hangs there.

Then the boy climbs the rope, coming into the glare of the sun. At that point he slides along the wire toward the tree or the wall, taking the direction recommended by the fakir, who has allowed for that, too. By the time the spectators manage to shield their eyes against the dazzling light, the boy is gone. All that remains for the fakir to do is give the rope an upward flip, disengaging the prong and making it drop down without the boy.

This version of the "Rope Trick" may be performed under different, perhaps more difficult conditions. According to one account, the ideal place is a tropical valley where fogs creep in between high hills and form a dense mist some twenty or thirty feet above the ground. The fakir has his wire rigged for just such an occasion. He tosses the pronged rope up into the thickening mist, the boy climbs it and scoots along the wire under cover of the fog, and the fakir then dislodges the rope for the customary climax.

The most practical application of this method is for the fakir to work before a small audience seated on a veranda with a low roof or overhanging awning. This effective version of the "Rope Trick" is attributed to a wily fakir who simply strung his wire high enough to be out of sight of his spectators, above the edge of the overhanging roof. After performing a routine of conventional conjuring, the fakir introduces the "Rope Trick" as a feature of his act. He tosses the rope into the air, and it stays up, of course, without anyone knowing why. The boy makes a quick climb and is immediately out of sight like the wire itself. He then heads for the bungalow roof, continuing over the top and in through the back door by the time the fakir has shaken the rope loose.

Such, at least, is the explanation that conforms to the testimony of baffled Britishers who have insisted that they witnessed the incredible "Rope Trick." Of course, they might have imagined the entire performance, or perhaps they were hypnotized. One guess is still as good as another so far as the fabulous Indian "Rope Trick" is concerned.

# PART 5

# ORIENTAL MAGIC

## Introduction

The marvels of the mysterious East have always been a dominant factor in the world of magic—and the most secret. Magicians of the Levant have perpetuated methods which date back to the ancient Egyptian wonder workers; similarly, Indian fakirs have passed their tricks on to successive generations, preserving the old traditions. The works of each form a subject in itself. But the magic of the Orient, most notably that of China and Japan, includes many mysteries that were for centuries unfathomable to the Western mind.

There is no need to relate the fanciful tales which Sir John Mandeville compiled in 1356 from the writings of many travelers whose chief qualities were imagination and exaggeration. The important point is that for more than four hundred years, most Europeans believed that Eastern wizards could light up half the globe with gigantic mirrors or transform themselves into cubes which rose in the air and remained suspended.

Fascination with such "witnessings," as Mandeville quaintly termed the mysteries of the Orient, eventually led Westerners to induce magicians of the Far East to visit Europe and America. When they came, however, their marvels proved far less spectacular than those described in the early accounts. Yet the magic they performed was highly mystifying; it impressed and influenced Western magicians, and such tricks as the Chinese "Linking Rings" and the Japanese "Thumb Tie" are presented today by American magicians to amazed audiences.

# The Boiling Water Ordeal

In the Middle Ages, the ordeal by boiling water was used to determine the innocence or guilt of certain criminals. This test required the accused man to dip his hand into a cauldron filled with boiling water and bring out a stone or weight from the bottom. According to one account, the man's arm was then bandaged for three days and if it proved to be fully healed he was regarded as innocent; otherwise he was declared guilty.

To a degree this ordeal was psychologically sound. A man who believed himself innocent would be apt to boldly thrust his hand into the water and come up promptly with the stone, while the culprit with a guilty conscience might hesitate and fumble in the process. In this action lay all the difference. It is a simple physical fact that one can avoid scalding by dipping one's hand quickly into boiling water and bringing it out just as fast; but any undue delay gives the very hot liquid time to take serious effect and produce a bad burn.

Many times, however, this principle would work in reverse. An innocent man might be worried and therefore hesitant, while a chronic culprit might brazenly submit to the test and come through unharmed. That was reason enough for the ordeal to fall from favor and eventually be discredited. But though the water test disappeared from the European scene, it continued to be performed elsewhere, especially in the Orient.

The boiling water ordeal is often exhibited in its own right, as a demonstration of incredible endurance—or magical power—on a spectacular scale. Travelers in India have told of fakirs who poured gallons of water into a trough above a blazing fire. As soon as bubbles appeared, indicating that the water had reached the boiling point, a nearly naked fakir would plunge into the trough. He submerged himself completely in the steaming bath, wallowing and splashing happily until the water was half gone, whereupon he climbed out triumphant and unharmed.

A similar ordeal is practiced by Japanese priests as one of their "miracles," in a rite called the Yubana, or Kugadochi; preceded by long and elaborate religious services, the exhibition is held in the presence of great crowds at festival celebrations. Water is heated in a huge cauldron until it boils over and the fire beneath sputters fiercely. The Shinto priest then lashes the hot water furiously with two stalks of bamboo, instantly surrounding himself with a terrific cloud of steam and shower, while the fire hisses and smokes. Yet the ordeal continues until the cauldron is empty, and when the steam clears away the "miracle man" is drenched with water, but quite uninjured. Sometimes the ordeal is performed by two or three priests at a time, who beat the boiling

water with their arms in frenzied excitement and are regarded as the recipients of divine favor.

Both the Hindu and the Shinto ordeals depend on the principle that heat always rises. When a deep vessel of cold water is heated, it will boil on top while it is still cool at the bottom. When the Hindu fakir plunged into the trough, he mixed the boiling liquid with the cooler water below, reducing the overall temperature to a degree where it was still very hot, but not dangerously so. Likewise, the Shinto priest cooled the water in the cauldron by heating it with bamboo stalks and sprinkling it through the air; the great volume of steam thus produced is very impressive, and harmless.

# The Ladder of Swords

Sword walking was an ancient Shinto ordeal known as Tsurigi Watari; but its secret was long ago learned by Japanese conjurers, so the priests abandoned it as a rite. Oriental performers later brought the mystery to Europe and America.

The feat is performed on a large stand, shaped like a stepladder; each rung is a sharp sword with the blade turned upward. The performer removes his shoes and hosiery, showing his bare feet. Next he exhibits the swords, calling attention to the keenness of their blades, and carefully replaces them on the rack, blade upward. He now sets one foot directly on the blade of the lowest weapon and raises his body until his entire weight presses on the foot resting on the sword. Then he places his other foot on the next rung and carefully shifts his weight. In this manner he climbs to the very top, whereupon he begins his perilous descent, while the audience looks on with amazement, expecting to see the performer suffer injury.

He reaches the bottom safely, however, and shows the soles of his feet marked with deep impressions made by the sword blades. It seems incredible that such an exhibition should be genuine, but the feat is accomplished without trickery or deception. The performer must

possess great nerve and a perfect sense of balance. He uses various means to harden the soles of his feet, and then practices for many months on swords with dull edges that cannot harm him.

When he places his foot on the first sword, he presses it slowly and firmly against the steel. He then rests a hand against the rack and shifts his weight to the foot. Every time he climbs a rung he exercises the utmost caution, always ready to rest his hand on the rack to steady himself. It is essential that the sword blades point straight upward. Everyone knows the keenness of a razor's edge; yet the blade of a razor can be pressed against the hand until it leaves an indentation without breaking the skin, so long as it does not turn. Likewise, the sword walker must never lose his balance because the slightest sideward motion of his foot might cause severe injury.

# Fire Walking

The ancient art of walking on fire has been practiced by various peoples and cultures, but in modern times it is considered chiefly an Oriental ritual, frequently witnessed in China, Japan, India, and other Eastern lands, including the Fiji Islands.

The fire-walk is usually performed in a trench filled with burning coals, a glowing pathway more than a dozen feet in length. The preparation of the fire is often a solemn and prolonged ceremony in itself; but when the proper moment arrives, the procedure is nearly the same in all instances.

The chief fire walker, whether he is the head man of the village or a member of some religious cult, steps barefooted on the red-hot coals and boldly strides to the far end of the blazing path without suffering the slightest harm. Other initiates follow his example, even though the heat rivals that of a fiery furnace. Sometimes even strangers are invited to join the remarkable parade of fire walkers, and they too come through unscathed.

This was particularly true in Japan, where for many years the fire-walk was a famous Shinto ritual known as Hi-watari. Visiting observers were amazed to see men, women, and children scampering barefoot through the blazing heat, each carrying a small charm called a "gohei" as their only protection against the fire.

Though many witnesses regard the fire-walk as an actual miracle, skeptics have long advanced a twofold explanation of the mystery. They claim that fire walkers rub a preparation such as alum on the soles of their feet for protection against burns. Next, fire walkers wait until the fire has died sufficiently for ashes to cover the red-hot coals. By stepping through steadily but swiftly, the fire walker tramples down these ashes and has only brief contact with the coals that are really hot enough to burn him.

There are facts to support these explanations. One authority has noted that in a province of China the peasants who participated

in the fire-walk customarily went barefoot, so their feet were already hardened. In Japan, fire walkers step in salt as part of the Shinto ritual, and the salt could contain a quantity of alum. In India, some fires are composed chiefly of twigs and light sticks that burn up rapidly and soon become mere embers.

Even when red-hot coals are used, the chief fire walker—who initiates the ritual—unquestionably tramples the coals along the central path, making it easier for those persons who follow. Also, spectators often imagine the fire to be hotter than it really is because the sides of the fire are heaped higher. But this merely draws oxygen from the center, where the temperature dwindles accordingly, so the walking is easier. However, these are special cases; in contrast, some fire-walks have been made under conditions so exacting as to preclude all trickery.

Fire walking remained much of an enigma until the 1930's, when British investigators persuaded a group of Oriental fire walkers to undergo a series of rigid tests in England. The first official test utilized a trench eleven and a half feet long, six feet wide, and nine inches deep. The fire required a ton of firewood, seven tons of oak logs, ten gallons of paraffin, and a load of charcoal to attain a surface temperature of 870° Fahrenheit.

The fire walker's feet were examined and found free of preparation. He strode boldly along the red-hot path, each foot touching the glowing coals twice. A few minutes later, he repeated the test and his feet remained uninjured. When two other persons tried the walk, both suffered blisters, one slight, the second severe.

A few years later, the same test was performed with another Oriental fire walker; however, this time the fire was hotter, about 1130° Fahrenheit. He came through unharmed, but persons who followed him were slightly burned. As a further experiment, the trench was lengthened to twenty feet and the fire was stepped up to 1460° Fahrenheit. The fire walker took six steps in the red-hot embers, and this time he suffered burns.

By then, the British investigators felt certain that they had finally found the real secret of fire walking. It depended on the total time of contact, which with a fire of high intensity could not be more than two steps for each foot, at an average time of less than a quarter-second apiece. Beyond that, the cumulative effect of repeated contact would result in burns. To double-check, they reverted to the shorter trench, but increased the heat to 1550° Fahrenheit. The fire walker went through unscathed.

The first fire walker later performed the feat at Radio City in New York; he was credited with accomplishing a near miracle in Ripley's "Believe It or Not," which stated that he traversed a fiery pit twenty feet long with a surface temperature of 1400° Fahrenheit. That was true; but according to news accounts of the fire-walk, the pit was divided in the center by a crosswise mound or dike of earth, where the walker stopped and rested briefly before continuing to the far end.

Thus the demonstration consisted of two separate walks of only ten feet each, exactly as performed in England, which fitted the findings already established by the British investigators.

# The Japanese Rice Mystery

Not all marvels of Oriental magic date back to ancient times; there are also modern wonders. The Japanese "Rice Mystery" is a feat of fairly recent origin. It was performed before small but select audiences at the beginning of the twentieth century, and invariably left them utterly nonplussed, but delighted.

As is often the case, the setting played an important part in the mystery's effectiveness. A bowing assistant ushered the spectators into a fair-sized room that had no stage whatever. There they were politely shown to cushions where they sat facing the magician, who rested on his knees surrounded by his equipment. His assistant was seated beside him, ready to produce items from lacquered boxes and hand them to the magician as needed.

The "Rice Mystery" was usually presented early in the act. After a few preliminary tricks to secure the audience's complete attention, the magician showed a square wooden container, several inches deep, and emphasized that it was absolutely empty. He filled this container to the brim with grains of rice, then set it on a slender, thin-topped stand and covered it with a silk flag. Striking the container with a closed fan, which he used instead of a wand, the magician commanded the rice to fly from the container invisibly and distribute itself among the members of the audience, bringing good luck to all those fortunate enough to receive some of it.

A whisk of the cloth, and the magician tilted the container forward, rattling his fan inside it to show that the rice had really flown. Having established that the container was completely empty, he then gestured to his audience, signifying that the rest was up to them.

With one accord, they began reaching into their pockets, sashes, hats and purses, smiling in amazement as they brought out small quantities of rice, exactly as the magician had predicted!

No one in the audience had been neglected, which made the mystery all the more incredible, and superstitious spectators would insist that the magician must be in league with Inari, the fox god, who alone could have managed such a miracle. Certainly, few tricks had more audience appeal than the "Rice Mystery," with everyone participating in the climax, yet the method was so simple that it added to the puzzlement.

The secret was in the wooden container: its bottom was slightly raised, and grains of rice had been glued to the depression underneath. When he exhibited the "empty" container, the magician was careful not to show its under side. When he filled the container, he began by scooping rice from a large lacquered box;

then, to save time, he dipped the container into the box and brought it out brimming with rice.

Actually, however, he inverted the container, and brought it out with its bottom up. After brushing any heaped grains back into the box, he showed the container as apparently full: the spectators saw the grains glued on the bottom, which they mistook for the top. When he covered the container, the magician again secretly turned it upside-down, so that when he whisked the cloth away he had simply to tilt the container forward and show that the rice had vanished.

Clever indeed, but the magical reappearance of the rice throughout the audience was still neater, for it was accomplished before the show had even started. Instead of calling on the fox god, the magician depended on the ushers who so politely bowed the audience to their places. Each usher had his pockets filled with rice and found a chance to drop some

95

into a spectator's pocket or elsewhere on his person.

By working the trick early in the act, the magician transported the vanished rice into the pockets of the spectators before they had time to learn that it had already been planted there, thus turning a simple magical effect into a baffling mystery.

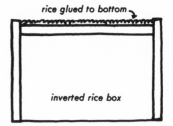

rice glued to bottom

inverted rice box

# The Water Fountain Mystery

If ever the fabled fantasies of the "Arabian Nights" were realized, it was through the performance of the "Water Fountain Mystery," a piece of modern Oriental magicianship that surpasses many of the ancient miracles. So impressively beautiful is the illusion of the Water Fountains that this mystery comprised an entire act in the British version of "Chu Chin Chow," one of the most elaborate musical spectacles of all time. The Fountains can be seen in movies of that show, but these fall far short of the real-life presentation as it appeared upon the stage. There, it was sheer magic.

Picture the scene as the curtains rise: Performers in Oriental costume are seated upon the steps of a raised platform, while attendants stand aside at respectful distances. A grand magician comes on stage and waves his wand above a vase resting on a table. Instantly, a jet of water spurts from the vase. The magician snatches at this little fountain and it disappears as though he had gathered it in his hand. He then throws it toward a lovely Oriental maiden fanning herself nearby, and the fountain immediately rises from the center of her fan.

Not only does the water flow there, it runs back and forth across the top of the fan, to the surprised delight of the other performers. The magician then snatches the fountain again from the fan and tosses it back to the vase, where it promptly reappears and continues to flow. Another maiden extends her fan, but

this time the fountain fails to travel all the way when the magician throws it, and returns instead to the vase. So he dips his wand into the water and carries the rising stream away on the wand's tip, transferring it to the fan.

As more fountains rise from the vase at the magician's command, he tosses them to other members of the troupe, and these ever-increasing fountains begin to spout from various parts of the stage. One jets from the top of a man's head, another on the point of an extended sword. An assistant gingerly pokes his finger into a fountain and carries it away on his fingertip. A sword is set edge-upward in an ornamental stand, and when a jet is thrown at it, the water rises from the center of the blade. Each time the magician captures a jet and throws it to the floor, another fountain springs up, until they are spouting everywhere, multiplying fantastically all over the stage. As colored lights play upon the scene, producing brilliant rainbows of flowing water, the Oriental music reaches a crescendo and the curtains close upon a shimmering tableau that lingers in the memory of all who have been fortunate enough to see it.

Though the Water Fountain Mystery is rather simple to perform, it is quite costly to produce because of the heavy equipment and elaborate preparation involved. Most of the streams that rise in such surprising fashion come from a back-stage tank set high up in the scenery so as to provide the needed water pressure. The water is piped to the performers on stage by assistants behind the scenes, who turn it on and off at certain cues.

What makes the trick so mystifying is the way in which the pipes are concealed or disguised. They all run under a carpet that covers the stage. One comes up through a leg and the center rod of the table which holds the vase, and this accounts for the first fountain of water. Another connects with a socket in the heel of the magician's shoe, and from there a pipe runs up under his costume and down his sleeve to his hand. This enables him to pluck the fountain from the vase and apparently carry it away at his fingertips. The magician can also connect the end of the pipe to a hollow wand which has an opening at the far end from which the jet reappears.

water tank

wall →

wig with hidden pipe

fan joined to socket
of pipe in sleeve

hose or pipe

carpet

pipe

97

Assistants have pipes running up beneath their costumes or behind chairs in which they are seated. One sleeve pipe connects with a swiveled extension on the back of a fan, which can be worked back and forth so that a jet appears to run along the fan's edge. Another comes up behind an assistant's neck and under a wig to the top of his head, where a tiny opening enables the water to emerge in a steady stream.

Two types of swords are used: One is hollow and the hilt connects to a sleeve pipe, like the wand, so the water can flow through to an opening in the sword tip. The other is an ordinary sword, but the stand on which it rests

has a pipe that can be swung behind the blade, so the water springs up there.

Other assistants carry rubber containers beneath their oversized Oriental jackets. These are connected to fans, wigs, and other objects from which fountains are made to spout. The rubber bags are filled with water, and by bowing and pressing them with one hand, the assistant forces a stream through the connecting hose. These assistants are able to rove about, carrying jets from one person to another, giving the Water Fountains that final touch of mystery which puzzles the keenest observer.

# The Dancing Duck

The following two tricks are favorites of Oriental street magicians; both coming out of India, they are important items in the reper-

toire of the itinerant fakirs and jadoo wallahs. The "Dancing Duck" requires a small bowl, or the hollow half of a cocoanut shell, and a

water

knotted hairs

tiny wooden duck. The magician brings the bowl from a bag and props it on some small stones. He fills the bowl with water, splashing some over the brim, and then sets the little duck afloat in it.

This accomplished, the jadoo wallah starts piping on a flute, and as the music swells, the duck begins to dance and dip its head. The piping shrills and the duck dives completely from sight as though annoyed, only to bob up serenely when the music pauses. The feat is repeated to the increasing wonderment of the onlookers, until the squatting magician finally plucks the duck from the water and hands it around for examination. He then empties the bowl, showing its interior quite free of any mechanical devices.

The very simplicity of this effect makes it seem like genuine magic; therefore it serves as a build-up to the fakir's more impressive and complex marvels. But the secret behind the effect of the "Dancing Duck" is also very simple. Attached to the duck by a dab of wax is a long thread, or a series of knotted hairs, that runs through a hole in the bottom of the bowl to the magician's flute. All these props are brought out together from the bag, so that it is easy for the jadoo wallah to set up his act.

The bowl is placed on a pile of small stones so the thread will run freely; and when the bowl is filled with water, some water is deliberately splashed on the ground around it, so that the slight leakage from the hole will not be noticed. As he pipes away on his flute, the jadoo wallah shifts position slightly, drawing the thread taut and relaxing it again, so that the duck dances, dives, and bobs up once more.

When he passes the duck around, the jadoo wallah detaches the wax end of the thread. The thread is then drawn down to the hole, or completely through it, when the bowl is finally emptied and shown. As the hole is too tiny to be noticeable, especially when drilled in a cocoanut shell, the empty bowl seems convincing evidence that no trickery was involved. Sometimes the jadoo wallah beats a tom tom instead of piping on a flute, but either way, the duck responds.

# The Bundar Boat

Quite as baffling as the "Dancing Duck" is the mystery of the "Bundar Boat," also known as the "Hubble Bubble." This trick originated in Bombay and spread to other parts of India, becoming a favorite with many wandering magicians throughout the Far East. The apparatus used consists of simple items: a miniature wooden boat, with a single seat or thwart across the center; an upright mast that fits into a hole in the thwart; and a hollow cocoanut shell, with a large hole fitting onto the upper end of the mast, and a small hole in the lower side.

At the start, the jadoo wallah fills the hollow cocoanut with water, puts it on the mast, and inserts the latter in the thwart. The boat is also filled with water, and the whole curious contrivance stands about one foot high. Squat-ting beside it, the jadoo wallah plays a tune on the flute or gourd. Suddenly, at his command, the action starts. From the small hole in the side of the cocoanut comes a jet of water that spurts down into the boat until the magician orders it to stop, which it does, just as suddenly as it began.

More piping ensues, and again the command to flow, then to stop. As before, the water spurts mysteriously. So it continues under the fakir's watchful eye, until finally the water in the cocoanut is almost exhausted. He then takes the device apart and packs away boat, mast and cocoanut, leaving his audience completely mystified.

This uncanny effect depends upon a simple hydrostatic principle, resembling the devices used in ancient pagan temples. How it found

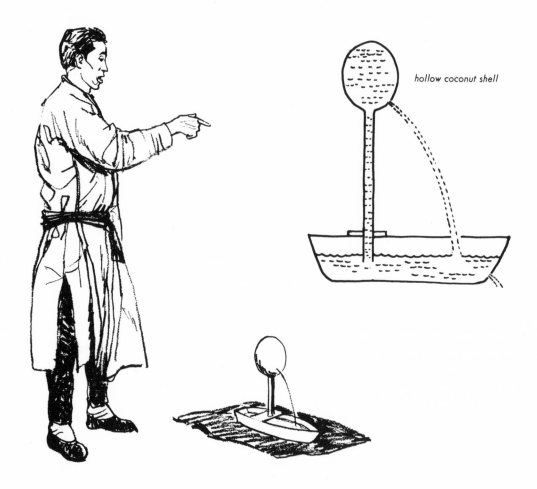

hollow coconut shell

its way into the repertoire of the jadoo wallah is an even greater mystery than the trick itself, but through generations these performers used it not only to baffle native audiences but European onlookers as well. Today, however, the secret is very well known.

The mast is hollow, forming a connection between the water in the boat and the cocoanut. When the cocoanut is filled and put in place upon the mast, water promptly flows down through the mast, but is stopped when it reaches the water in the boat. No water flows from the small hole in the side of the cocoanut, because there is no way for air to enter the cocoanut and replace it.

Unknown to the onlookers, the boat has an even smaller hole in the bottom. Water trickles through this hole but is unnoticed because the jadoo wallah has purposely spilled water around the boat, as he did in the "Dancing Duck" trick. Very gradually, the level of the water in the boat goes down until it comes below the bottom of the hollow mast. Then air goes up through the mast, and water pours from the hole in the side of the shell.

This is only half the trick. The shell is turned so that the water pours down into the boat, bringing the water level up to the thwart. That cuts off the air from the bottom of the mast, and the flow from the cocoanut stops. As more water leaks from the small hole in the boat, the level again is lowered and the mystery repeats itself automatically.

The jadoo wallah plays this to perfection, timing his commands to the self-working device and creating the impression that his control over inanimate objects borders on the miraculous.

# The Spikes and The Stone

In the latter years of vaudeville, an Egyptian fakir astonished American audiences with an exhibition that many took for a miracle—or for a marvel of Oriental magic. He allowed a committee to examine a bed made of many long spikes, each one sharp enough to scratch a person's finger. Then he calmly shed his Egyptian robe and lowered his broad bare back upon the spikes, resting there serenely. Remarkable as this was, however, much more was to follow.

Two assistants brought forward a huge, heavy stone and placed it upon the fakir's chest and stomach. That put still more pressure on his back, but he remained unperturbed. Then one assistant lifted a sledge hammer and began to strike at the enormous stone with forcible blows that would seem to impale

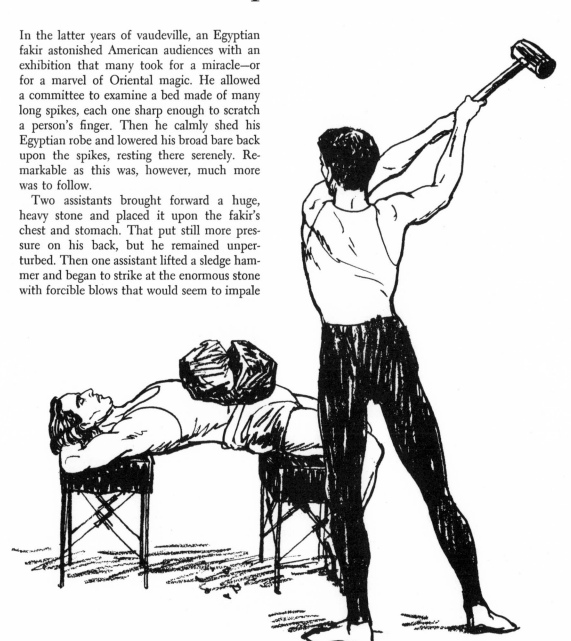

the recumbent fakir upon the spikes beneath him. At every ringing blow the audience winced with sympathetic pain; but the assistant continued to hammer away until the force of his strokes broke the stone completely in half, so that its parts fell to the stage.

Finally, while the audience gasped in disbelief, the fakir rose slowly and majestically from his bed of spikes as though arousing himself from a deep trance. He swelled his chest and slapped his hands against it to prove that the crushing blows had done him no harm. Then he showed his back, which the awed onlookers expected to be streaked with bloody gashes. It was not even scratched, but the imprints of dozens of spike points deeply penetrated the fakir's flesh, proving that the test had been real to the last degree.

It was accepted as a display of magic—of superhuman power to withstand torture. But the fakir's demonstration actually combined two old tricks used in India by Sadhus and other holy men, who frequently lie on beds of sharp spikes to show their disregard for pain and discomfort. Curiously, the greater the number of spikes, the more comfortable the bed is apt to be, as the fakir's weight is more widely distributed. A man can press his finger firmly against a single spike point without suffering any harm; and when the weight of the entire body is spread out over dozens of such points, the average is reduced to less than finger pressure. The fakir in this case had merely to lie down carefully and evenly, keeping his body entirely immobile.

The addition of the heavy stone considerably increased the weight and pressure, but the fakir had allowed for that. So his situation remained the same up to the hammering of the stone.

This involved the second trick, an old strongman stunt known as "the man of iron." This demonstration, which has often been exhibited in sideshows, actually requires no supernatural power or even special strength. It can be performed by any man who is capable of supporting the weight of the stone upon his body.

It is a practical experiment in inertia. The larger the stone, the easier the trick. If the stone is too small the drives of the sledge hammer may carry through and injure the performer; but a large stone absorbs the force of the blows and renders them virtually negligible. Eventually the stone cracks apart, marking the finish of this fantastic act, and the longer it takes the more effective it is.

In fact, when imitators of the Egyptian fakir sprang up, as was common in vaudeville at that time, one act used a heavy steel anvil instead of the big stone. This was particularly effective because the heavy anvil absorbed the strokes of the small sledge hammer and the assistant continued to beat out the "anvil chorus" until the recumbent and supposedly entranced fakir decided that the climax had been reached. He then gave the signal to end the hammer strokes and remove the anvil so that he could rise and take his bow.

# Mind Over Matter

Among the marvels which Egyptian fakirs have performed both in Europe and America, there are several that seem to require extraordinary mental control over actions which are ordinarily involuntary. The fakirs themselves attribute this "mind power" to some occult and magical force, but various scientific observers have classed it as auto-hypnosis. Neither of these theories fully covers the case, as some-

times an element of trickery may be involved. For soon after the Egyptian fakirs popularized their miraculous feats, a host of imitators sprang up who presented most of the same marvels in practically the same style. Hence the line of demarcation between the true and the false is quite thin, as a study of the tests themselves will show.

To demonstrate his ability at mind control,

the fakir first invites a committee on the stage at the beginning of the performance, and asks someone to hold his wrist and note his pulse beats. During this procedure, the fakir's eyes take on a faraway stare indicating that he has assumed a state of trance. Gradually his pulse beats slacken and finally fade away almost entirely, much to the amazement of the man who holds his wrist. Coming out of his trance, the fakir immediately brings his pulse beats up to the normal rate. He repeats the test with different persons holding his wrists, raising and lowering his pulse beats at request until the entire committee is satisfied as to his uncanny ability.

He then proceeds with a more spectacular demonstration that convinces the entire audience as well. Pressing one hand against the back of his neck and the other upon his forehead, the fakir forces himself into a deeper trance. His manager then instructs committee members to thrust long hat pins and skewers through the fakir's shoulders, his jaws and cheeks, and finally the fakir allows the fleshy portion of his throat to be pierced with a long thin dagger blade.

None of these implements are faked. The fakir would scorn to use "trick" daggers or bodkins like those of the medieval conjurers. Pins, skewers, and dagger are all examined,

during and after the experiment. But this is not all: to make the miracle totally convincing, the skewers are reserved until the finish. So far, the fakir has apparently been unharmed and there has been no flow of blood from his wounds. The spectators assume that this was because he virtually stopped his heart beat, as he earlier demonstrated with the pulse test. The manager stresses the fakir's trance condition and announces that now the miracle man will cause blood to flow or stop at request. The committee calls for the flow of blood, and as the fakir promptly draws a skewer from his cheek, the wound begins to bleed. With the next skewer, they ask the fakir to control the flow, and when he removes the skewer no blood appears. This test is repeated skewer by skewer, always in accordance with the committee's wishes.

Having fully convinced both committee and audience of his supreme control, the fakir submits to further torture tests. Finally he presses his neck and forehead still more forcibly and goes into a complete cataleptic trance, falling back into the waiting arms of his assistants. The committee, which may include medical men, finds that both his breathing and his heart-beats have almost completely ceased. In this state of coma the fakir is placed in a coffin which is sealed and covered with earth for a stipulated period of an hour or more. The lack of air does not bother the fakir, for when the coffin is finally opened the miracle man rises from his comatose state and resumes his normal poise.

Whatever the actual or reputed powers of the more .skilled fakirs, clever trickery and constant practice can account for the performances described above. Pulse stopping may be accomplished with the aid of a small rubber ball or block of wood, which is concealed under the fakir's arm. To cause his pulse to die away, he merely presses his arm against the block of wood. Another technique is for the performer to wear a high stiff neckband and press it downward with his chin, against his collarbone. With either method, sufficient practice can enable the fakir to con-

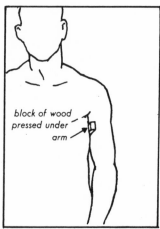

block of wood pressed under arm

trol his pulse in a most convincing fashion.

When hatpins and skewers are thrust into his flesh, the fakir first presses upon the nearest artery and temporarily restrains the flow of blood. Then he relaxes and immediately pushes the skewer straight through the skin. The operation is painful on the surface but the performer soon trains himself to withstand it. Before the dagger is thrust through his throat, the fakir draws the flesh forward between his thumb and fingers, so that the blade penetrates only the fleshy part.

When the implements are removed, they are drawn out slowly to enable the wound to swell, thus preventing any flow of blood. In removing a skewer from his cheek, the performer can cause blood to flow by the simple expedient of drawing the skewer out more rapidly.

To present the cataleptic test, the average fakir combines the simple pulse-stopping test with slow breathing which is reduced to an absolute minimum. When sealed in the coffin he continues to breathe very slowly and lightly, consuming as little oxygen as possible. He is also careful not to move about, as any activity also uses up oxygen and he must depend upon the original supply to see him through the allotted time. This is tested beforehand, and by frequent practice, the fakir is gradually able to prolong the time of burial. An hour and a half is regarded as the outside limit of this test as performed by the most proficient fakirs.

# Buried Alive

One of the darkest secrets of the Orient is the mystery of suspended animation—the temporary withdrawal from life. Egyptian fakirs have presented "living burials," in which the coffin containing the fakir is placed in an actual grave and covered with earth, or the casket is sealed in a water-tight container and lowered to the bottom of a river. Such feats are very sensational when performed before thousands of spectators: suspense increases until the coffin is unearthed or brought to the surface of the river and the fakir emerges alive. People are overawed by these cataleptic demonstrations, even when the entire performance runs as little as half an hour. The secret of short time burial, however, is the nerve and stoicism of the individual, who, if he remains quiet and in a semi-conscious condition, bordering on actual

hypnosis, can exist for a surprisingly long time on very little air, as previously described.

But there are stories of Oriental mystics who allowed themselves to be buried alive for days or even weeks at a time. Hindus frequently attribute this ability to Samadhi, the highest stage of Yoga whereby the soul leaves the body but remains attached to the inanimate human form by a slender invisible cord, which enables it to return later.

According to one account, a Yogi named Haridas was buried in Lahore, India, in 1837, while in a state of suspended animation, and remained underground for forty days. A few years later, a similar case was reported in the native state of Jaisalmer, where an entranced fakir was placed in a grave beneath a stone building measuring only twelve by eight feet.

hidden exit

secret tunnel →

105

This tomb was covered with heavy slabs and the house itself was walled up and placed under constant guard for a full month. When the fakir was dug up, he was found to be very much alive, though somewhat weak, and stated that next time they could bury him for a year if they so desired. Apparently everyone was satisfied with his feat, as there is no record of a repeat performance by that particular fakir.

These extended living burials are not confined to India. Around 1913, a British investigator named Harry Price witnessed the conclusion of such a burial in Tunis, North Africa. Price learned that ten days before, a party of Americans had buried a fakir at his own request and that they were now about to dig him up. Price was on hand for the event and states that the disinterred fakir seemed to be dead but began to revive after thirty minutes, and within an hour he was apparently his normal self. This is one of the rare instances of a firsthand account of an extended living burial by a highly competent witness. Unfortunately, Price was not there at the start, only at the finish, so he was unable to report on any trickery that may have transpired earlier.

This is an essential point, because whether or not human beings are capable of suspended animation, trickery is employed in many such demonstrations. Cases of pretended Samadhi have been reported along with supposedly genuine feats. In fact, some authorities claim that there are far more fakers than fakirs where this performance is concerned.

Fraudulent burials are usually held in the smaller towns of India. A large hole is dug in the ground, and the fakir, under supposed hypnotic influence, is placed in a wooden coffin which is lowered into the deep pit. Earth is thrown in upon him and packed tight. Constant guard is kept over the spot to make sure the fakir is not removed. At the end of several days, the grave is opened and the apparently lifeless fakir is revived in the usual fashion.

The grave is filled and the fakir goes his way triumphantly, with another "miracle" to his credit.

Actually, there is no miracle at all. The whole act is prepared beforehand by the fakir and a group of accomplices. When the place has been set for the burial, the fakir spends a few days preparing himself for his ordeal. This gives his confederates time to dig an underground passage from a hut or tent nearby to the exact spot of the grave.

When the grave is dug, nobody notices the concealed passage, as a narrow wall of earth has been left between it and the end of the grave. When the fakir is buried, he waits only until he hears the earth begin to thud on his coffin. He then opens a loose end of the coffin and pushes his way through to the underground passage, where he crawls to the hut occupied by his friends. They conceal him there until the time comes to reopen the grave. The fakir then crawls back through the tunnel and resumes his place in the coffin so that he is unearthed with it. His confederates lose no time in shoveling dirt back into the grave, thus hiding any evidence of the secret passage.

One such case was reported in the district of Surat, India, where the fakir promised to provide the added miracle of "projecting" his "astral body" to a town two hundred miles away, so that he would be seen there in person on the fifteenth day of his one-month burial. Although Yogis of a higher order claim such power during Samadhi, the governor doubted that this Yogi could perform the double miracle, particularly as it would take him just about two weeks to go each way on foot. So the guards apprehended the fakir's confederates immediately after he had been buried and the upper end of the secret tunnel was uncovered beneath a large water jar in their camp nearby. The fakir was taken into custody on his way out, so the fraud was exposed at its very start.

# PART 6

# SECRETS *of* STAGE MAGIC

## Introduction

Magic, as we have seen, has always had a strong element of entertainment. With the rise of the modern theater, this dramatic quality came into its own and there developed the art of the stage magician. The popularity of pantomimes, with their transformations and other surprising effects, encouraged magicians to desert the small halls and the booths of country fairs and to venture into ambitious theatrical projects.

Some built their own magical theaters, specially fitted for the production of new and spectacular mysteries. Others carried tons of equipment on extensive tours, since the trend called for more elaborate apparatus that could be seen and appreciated by larger audiences. As stagecraft techniques advanced, old methods were discarded and big illusions came into vogue.

The vaudeville era, with its incessant demand for novelty, offered profitable opportunities for specialty acts. This led to the development of many new and unusual magical effects that are still being performed today. Examples of both old and new will be found in the section that follows.

# The Sword Stabbing Mystery

From the earliest days of magical performances, wizards have demonstrated their immunity to dangerous weapons; this popular mystery of the Middle Ages finds its modern counterpart in an ingenious feat of stage magic. The magician brings on stage a pair of swords, hands one to an assistant, and invites him to a fencing match. After a few feints and parries, the magician makes a sudden thrust and drives the blade of his sword straight through his opponent's body, so that the point emerges from the other man's back.

Ordinarily this would prove fatal, but a magician is always capable of rectifying his errors. He places one hand on the assistant's shoulder and with the other hand gives the sword a hard wrench, bringing it completely free. Then the assistant goes his way, unharmed by the brief misadventure.

The trick involves two factors. The sword blade is made of flexible metal, and the assistant wears beneath his jacket a curved metal sheath that fits around one side of his body. This sheath is the equivalent of a scabbard which holds the sword, except that it is open at both ends, and these openings are concealed in the ornamental braid work of the assistant's jacket.

During the duel, the magician seeks the opening of the sheath with the point of his sword. Once he finds it and fixes the point there, he can deliver his thrust. The pliable blade travels around through the tubular sheath to emerge from the assistant's back. A quick draw on the sword brings the blade out again, and the trick is done.

In another version of the sword stabbing mystery, the magician finds that the blade is stuck so tightly in the assistant's body that its removal is impossible; so he lets it stay as it is, assuring his helper that no harm can come from it. Of course it is a slight inconvenience to go about with a sword protruding through his body, but he should be grateful that he is no worse off. The act concludes with that comment.

It is an improvement over the older trick, because in the original method the sword had

to be removed from the assistant's body before the audience realized that it was slightly shorter than at the start, due to its curvature. In the newer version, the length of the sword does not change. The assistant can turn around, displaying the sword back and front, while the magician measures it with the other sword and finds them to be exactly alike in length.

This effect is accomplished with the aid of a short blade already in the sheath, its point set to emerge from the assistant's back. When the magician drives home the original sword, its flexible blade encounters the hidden segment and pushes it out ahead. That makes up for the difference in length, but the sword cannot be withdrawn from the assistant's body as the point would remain in sight, still projecting from his back.

Some magicians handle this by having the assistant face the audience, then pulling the sword free from the front without letting him show his back again. But it is more effective to have him walk off stage, still impaled by the sword, as though pondering over his strange dilemma.

# The Living Head

More than a century ago, London theater audiences were horrified and amazed by a truly gruesome illusion called the "Living Head." It was set in a torture chamber beneath an old castle; there, in a stone-walled alcove surmounted by an archway, stood a simple three-legged table. On top of this table were two skulls facing a human head that lay tilted and lifeless upon a plate.

At one side of the alcove, a masked executioner leaned upon a long sword; at the other,

a wizard crouched above a brazier, casting magic powders into its flames. The fire turned from red to green, then delivered a puff of smoke with a pungent aroma; and under the spell of the magician's incantation, the head stirred and came to life. It blinked its eyes, tilted its chin upward, and after coughing from the fumes, it began to converse with the wizard.

While the audience listened, spellbound, the head told how, when alive, it had owned

111

great riches, and where this treasure could now be found. But before it finished speaking, the effect of the magic powder wore off, the spell broke, and the head drooped back upon the plate. Then the curtains closed, marking the end of the mysterious and melodramatic scene.

To the audience, the mystery was baffling indeed because the table was devoid of any drapery and its top was only a few inches thick. One could therefore see completely beneath the table, clear to the back of the stone-walled cell. Nor was the head a mechanical device, for its actions and its speech were positively lifelike and too varied to be duplicated by a mere automaton.

Here was an illusion really "done with mirrors," and done so ingeniously that people unfamiliar with the method would be mystified by the trick today. A pair of mirrors ran from the front leg of the table to the two back legs, completely filling the space between the table-top and the floor. The mirrors were set at right angles to each other, so they reflected the side walls of the alcove.

The alcove's rear wall was exactly the same distance from the center of the table and was designed to match the sides. Thus, when the mirrors were properly registered, their reflections appeared as a continuation of the wall

behind the table, creating the illusion of being able to see clear through beneath the table. This illusion works at any angle provided the spectators do not sit too far to either side; but the walls of the alcove were extended sufficiently forward to cut off a direct view into the mirrors.

An assistant sat in the V-shaped space behind the mirrors, with his head projecting up through a sectional collar made to resemble a plate. His face was made up in ghastly fashion to represent the living head that "died" before it could deliver its important message. The wizard and the executioner were careful to stay out in front of the alcove, as their legs would have been reflected in the mirrors if they had approached the sides of the table too closely.

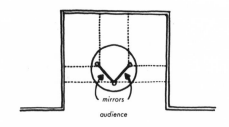

# The Girl In The Swing

Early in the era of mirror illusions, the famous "Living Head" was rivalled by the even more ingenious illusion of the "Half Lady." The head and torso of a young lady were seen upon a circular platform with three short legs; this in turn stood upon a table with a thin, undraped top. People could see beneath both platform and table, but what distinguished this trick was that the table had a fourth leg at the rear corner.

This seemed to rule out the use of mirrors running from the front to the side legs of the table, because in hiding the girl's body from

the waist down, these would also have cut off view of the rear leg. Yet the mirrors were there, as in the "Living Head" illusion, reflecting the sides of the alcove so it would appear as the back. But at the front corners of the alcove were two ornamental pillars. Behind each of these was a dummy leg, so situated that it was reflected as if it were beneath the rear corner of the table.

Spectators at the right saw the dummy leg on their side; spectators at the left saw the leg on the other side. All were equally deceived, but the illusion was difficult to set up,

112

and people were becoming suspicious of tables anyway. So a new illusion was developed and displayed as the "Girl in the Swing."

The swing was like a trapeze, painted white and set in a curtain-lined alcove. On the swing was a living woman whose body terminated at the waist. The background was in complete darkness, but the swing itself was brilliantly illuminated by bright lights equipped with metal reflectors, and the performer was able to wave his arms beneath the swing while the "half lady" blithely held on to the supporting chains and smiled at the audience.

Her smile was the most difficult part of the

trick, for the girl was in a very strained and uncomfortable position. Only her head, shoulders and arms were actually visible to the audience; the rest of the "half-body" was a dummy form encased in a type of corset or foundation garment extending downward from the girl's bust. Her own body and legs were garbed in a tight-fitting costume which matched the dark color of the background curtain. The girl reclined face downward in a special hammock running straight back to a strong metal rest fixed to the wall behind the curtain, to which her feet were firmly strapped.

The dazzle produced by the reflected lights

contrasted sharply with the deep gloom inside the alcove, so that the girl's figure blended into the darkness around her. This prevented anyone who looked in from an angle from seeing her prone form behind the swing, while persons who avoided the glare by gazing straight from the front could only see the girl's "half-body," which blocked any view of her real form beyond.

The stage set was a boxed alcove, much like a cabinet, but with a top to insure the necessary darkness. The trapeze hung a few feet from the front, and the remaining depth of the setting was determined by the length of the girl's body in the hammock. A neat and convincing effect was added when the "half lady" lifted herself slightly upward by gripping crossbars between the pairs of chains that supported the swing. This lifted the dummy form and enabled the performer to pass a sword blade between it and the trapeze, a touch that proved that mirrors were out of the question.

However, the "Girl in the Swing" also had its limitations, as it could never be shown on a large stage. Like the earlier "Half Lady" it was relegated to sideshows and dime museums. Then, London was suddenly captivated by a full-stage version of the swing illusion called the "Girl in the Balloon." The curtain rose to disclose an imitation balloon with a swing beneath, carrying a circular platform with a living half lady.

The stage was brilliantly lighted, the girl was certainly alive, and to top it all, the balloon glided over the audience while the half lady tossed flowers to the spectators. The balloon then drifted back to the stage, the curtains closed, and the audience believed that they had really seen a living half lady. Actually, they had.

The girl in the balloon was the victim of a railroad accident which had necessitated the amputation of both her legs. A theatrical producer had hit upon the idea of staging a real half lady, and the "Girl in the Balloon" was the result, to their mutual profit. Audiences were unable to fathom the mystery, and after several successful seasons, the "Girl in the Balloon" retired from the stage with a sizeable fortune.

# The Floating Lady

To defy the law of gravity, to suspend a human being in mid-air! This has been the dream of wonder workers through the centuries. It was partly attained by Hindu fakirs, who appeared to rise using an upright cane as their only support; and spirit mediums often claimed that they could float about a darkened seance room. But the levitation of a living person on a fully lighted stage before an entire theater audience was achieved through the triumph of modern magic.

In this remarkable illusion, the magician introduces a young lady attired in a loose, flowing gown. He hypnotizes the girl, and she falls back into the arms of a waiting assistant. Another assistant helps place her on a couch in the center of the stage, facing the audience. The magician, standing behind the couch, makes magnetic passes above her recumbent form. Slowly, steadily, the girl's rigid body rises upward until she is completely above the couch and apparently asleep in mid-air.

The assistants then take away the couch, showing all clear below. With a few more magnetic passes, the girl rises almost to the level of the magician's shoulders. As she rests there, an assistant brings a solid hoop to the magician and he passes it completely about and around the floating lady, from head to foot, in every direction. The magician returns the hoop to the assistant, who carries it down to the audience for examination.

Then the magician reverses his magnetic passes and the floating lady slowly descends, while the assistants place the couch beneath her. Once again on the couch, she is lifted

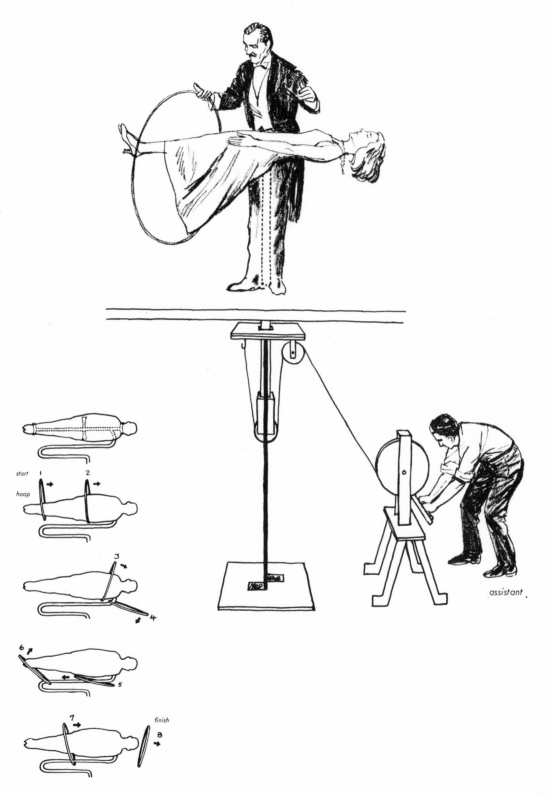

start
1
hoop

2

3
4

6
5

7
finish
8

assistant.

115

by the assistants and is brought from her trance at a snap of the magician's fingers.

While good showmanship is necessary for an effective performance of the "Floating Lady," the real secret is a combination of ingenious mechanical features. These were developed into a levitation which fulfilled all the basic requirements of the feat. The girl rests on a skeleton framework set in the couch, with a metal bar extending through a narrow, well-camouflaged slit in the back of the couch. The bar continues in a double curve resembling an elongated gooseneck, ample enough for the magician to move into the rear and larger portion.

Below the stage is an upright rod operated by a crank and cable. This rod comes up through the stage floor and engages a socket in the end of the curved metal bar. An assistant begins cranking the drum after the magician has stepped behind the couch, so the upright rod is concealed by the magician's legs as it emerges through the stage. That part of the cranking is rapid, but once the gooseneck is hooked up to the rod, the action is slower, for now begins the real "lift."

Thus the girl rises from the couch. Her flowing costume hides the supporting frame beneath her. Once the curved bar is clear of the couch, the magician pauses so the couch can be removed. The girl rises further under the "magnetic influence," until the magician calls for his hoop. He passes the hoop around the girl from her head almost to her feet, until stopped by the curved bar; then he swings it around her feet and carries the hoop in back, until the next curve blocks its passage. A swing around the girl's head, and he can sweep the hoop clear beyond her feet. These maneuvers are shown step by step in the accompanying diagram.

At the magician's cue, the assistant below stage reverses the crank, lowering the "floating lady" to the couch. When the assistants on the stage lift her from the couch, they take enough time for the upright rod to be cranked down through the floor. The magician is then free to step from behind the couch and de-hypnotize the girl.

The levitation has been presented in this form on large stages under the most exacting conditions, and it has also been shown on small outdoor platforms. However, it has two limitations: The magician cannot walk away while the girl is in mid-air; and he cannot raise her higher than his shoulders without revealing the upright rod. There is also a mechanical problem if the facilities below the stage are inadequate for installation of the lifting device.

This difficulty has been overcome in some instances by working the illusion very close to a curtain, behind which is a lifting device set on the stage itself. In this case, the curtain hides the lift, and no upright rod is needed. Instead, the horizontal bar extends from the couch, through a slit in the curtain, directly to the lift, which is anchored by heavy cables attached to the stage. This device works nicely, except on a deep stage where the levitation is performed so close to the back-drop that it arouses suspicion. To offset that, a still more elaborate form of levitation has been devised, utilizing thin wires that cannot be seen against the pattern of the back curtain. Although it is much more complex mechanically, the operation is similar to the basic method as described.

# Sawing A Woman In Half

The most sensational mystery of its day was "Sawing a Woman in Half," which was presented by many famous magicians of the vaudeville era and has been a main feature of magical programs ever since. In effect it rivals the most fantastic tales of the "Arabian Nights." An oblong box is exhibited upon a raised platform. Doors are opened in the front,

back, and top, and a girl is placed in the box.

There, she extends her head and hands through holes in one end of the box and her feet through openings in the other end. Spectators hold the girl's hands and feet, the doors are closed, and the magician, aided by an assistant, begins to saw the box in half with a huge cross-cut saw.

They saw straight downward through the center of the box, and spectators begin to shriek and faint when the saw nears the girl's body. But they continue sawing until they reach the platform. Then two square slabs are pushed down in grooves between the severed halves of the box, and one section is slid away from the other, separating them entirely. But the girl's head and hands still extend from one end and her feet from the other.

The magician walks between the two halves of the box to prove there can be no connection between them. They are then pushed together again; the slabs are taken out; the top of the box is removed and the girl lifted out, uninjured by her harrowing experience.

There are two methods of performing this illusion, both requiring a hollow platform. In the simpler version, the box is considerably shorter than the girl, so the doors must be closed before she extends her head, hands and feet from the ends of the box. Otherwise spectators will see that her knees are bent so that her body is hunched.

The box itself is bottomless, and the center portion of the platform is divided lengthwise into two sections. These are hinged, front and back, so they swing downward and inward when the girl rests her full weight on them. The girl stretches her body as she sags down in the platform, so there is no visible change in the position of her head, hands and feet.

There is a hinged board set upright inside the back of the box, occupying the space between the rear doors. This is dropped forward by an assistant so it forms a center strip in the platform. This hides the girl's body and also acts as a protection against the sawing that immediately follows.

The box is sawed down to the platform, and the slabs are inserted in grooves so the sections of the box can be separated without revealing their emptiness. During the separation, the girl stretches herself still further, allowing enough space for the magician to step between the sections. The various stages of the trick are clearly shown in the accompanying diagrams.

After the sawing, the process is reversed. The halves of the bottomless box are pushed together, the slabs are removed from their slots, the center strip is raised by an assistant while the doors are being opened and the girl is lifted from the box.

This simpler version has one obvious weakness. The sections of the box cannot be drawn very far apart, so the magician must squeeze one foot ahead of the other as he goes between. That is overcome in a more elaborate method

using two girls: One is placed visibly in the bottomless box; the other girl has already been concealed in the platform under the box.

After the visible girl goes into the box, the doors are closed and she doubles her knees above her body so she occupies the "head" section only. That portion of the platform is solid, enabling the girl to maintain her position while she extends her head and hands through that end of the box. Meanwhile, the girl in the platform pushes her legs up through a small trap in the "foot" section of the box so she can thrust her feet through that end.

As in the other method, the magician saws down the center of the box until he reaches the platform. The girls keep their positions, as shown in the diagram. However, after the slabs are in place, the "head" end of the box can be slid several feet along the platform, which was built with added length for that very purpose. This separates the two sections so widely that it would be impossible for anyone to stretch across the intervening space.

After the sections are slid together again and the slabs are removed, the platform is swung around to show all sides, enabling the girl in the platform to withdraw her feet from the "foot" section of the box while the original girl extends hers instead. The switch is made while that end of the box is turned away from the audience.

# Marching Under Water

One of the greatest modern water mysteries was frequently performed at the mammoth New York Hippodrome, once the city's largest playhouse with the unique feature of an actual lake beneath its stage. During one season, the opera "Pinafore" was produced on a real ship floating on the Hippodrome's artificial lagoon. Many spectacular water pageants were presented on the lake, and it was during some of these that the great mystery was introduced.

Beneath the lake was an imaginary land presumably peopled by amphibious human beings. Three rows of soldiers clad in armor would march forward to the lake, down a flight of steps, and disappear into its depths, row after row. Not a bubble arose; only a ripple remained on the surface. An entire chorus vanished and not one returned—a mystery that left audiences utterly amazed.

In other pageants, the spectacle was reversed, and people appeared suddenly upon the surface of the lake. On other occasions, swimmers dived from high boards into the lake and never came up. All this intrigued the

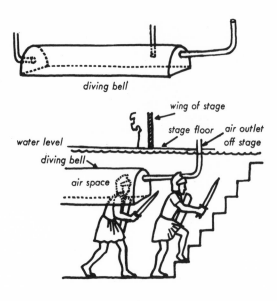

diving bell

wing of stage

stage floor

air outlet off stage

water level

diving bell

air space

demonstrated by filling a bowl with water, then inverting a drinking glass and pushing it down into the bowl. No water will enter the glass, but its pressure will compress the air to some degree. This, however, is comparatively slight except at great depths. A diving bell is simply a huge bowl large enough to contain several persons.

At the Hippodrome a long narrow bell was used extending clear across the tank, as shown in the accompanying illustration. It was affixed to metal uprights, allowing a four-foot space beneath it. The weight of their armor enabled the men to march down to the bottom of the tank, holding their breath while they stooped beneath the diving bell and came up into it. Once there they followed the diving bell to one end, where a flight of steps led up behind the scenes. Each row of men moved out to allow space for the next. The bell was equipped with two pipes, an inlet for fresh air at one end and an outlet at the other. Fresh air was constantly pumped in, keeping the bell ready for occupancy at all times.

Persons who appeared on the surface of the lake took their places in the bell beforehand. Divers who disappeared into the lake simply came up beneath the bell or swam under water to the steps leading off stage.

huge audiences that frequently filled the Hippodrome to capacity. As a result the lake eventually became a feature attraction of nearly every Hippodrome show.

The secret of "marching under water" consisted of a specially constructed diving bell. The principle of the diving bell can be easily

# Underwater Escape

Escape acts were extremely popular during the vaudeville era, and one of the most exciting was the "packing box escape." A committee was invited on the stage to examine a solid packing case. The escape artist was then handcuffed and placed in the box. The box's lid was firmly nailed, and it was pushed into a cabinet. Soon the wizard emerged, free of his handcuffs, and the packing box was found to be as tightly nailed as before.

When newly devised escapes became popular, performers gave the packing box escape a new twist, turning it into a sensation of its own. It was presented as an outdoor attraction

to bring audiences to the theater. The escape artist was handcuffed and nailed inside the packing box as usual; then a chain was fastened around the box and it was lowered from a pier or bridge into a river. Sometimes thousands of people lined the shore, watching in breathless suspense while the seconds ticked into minutes, until it seemed a miracle that the escape artist should come out alive.

Suddenly, after long moments, a head bobbed to the surface, bringing gasps and hurrahs from the crowd. It was the wonder worker, free of his shackles and the box, swimming to the safety of the shore. When the box was hauled up from the river and pried open, the handcuffs were found inside, still locked.

This is really a double escape, first from the handcuffs, and then from the box. The performer uses handcuffs of a standard pattern, with duplicate keys concealed in his bathing suit. Thus he is shackled and placed in the box, and while the lid is being nailed on he obtains the keys and releases himself from the handcuffs. That leaves him free to work on the box by the time it has been lowered into the water.

The box has been specially prepared for the escape. Each side of the box is formed by two long boards; these are held together by nails driven through the ends of the box into the ends of the boards. On one side, the upper board is held by two nails only, one at each end, close to the top. The other nails have been removed and replaced by short ones which barely enter the ends of the special

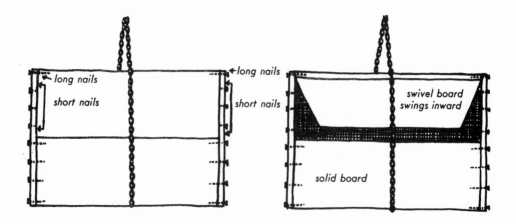

long nails

short nails

long nails

short nails

swivel board swings inward

solid board

board. All the boards have air holes so the performer can breathe during the early part of the escape. By inserting a finger in an air hole he is able to swing the lower edge of the trick board inward, the two nails at the top acting like a pivot or a hinge. He then works his head, shoulders and finally his body out through the opening. Once clear, he again inserts a finger in the air hole and swivels the loose board back in place. It is then only a case of waiting until he is almost out of breath before rising to the surface.

In some boxes, two pieces of pliable metal are fitted into secret slots between the edges of the loose board and the one beneath it. This holds the two boards firmly in position so that the box can stand considerable ex-

amination prior to the escape. In this case, the escape artist has a thin metal wedge concealed in his bathing suit and uses this to pull the strips free as the box reaches the water, thus releasing the loose board. Often an escape artist allows a local lumber yard to build a packing box according to his specifications. After the box is delivered at the theater, the long nails are removed and the short ones put in their place.

Houdini made a great feature of the underwater box escape and during one season performed it regularly at the New York Hippodrome, where the box was lowered into the artificial lake beneath the stage. This combined the effect of the theatrical presentation with that of the outdoor spectacle.

# Houdini's Vanishing Elephant

By its sheer size alone, the famous "Vanishing Elephant" spectacle presented by Houdini at the New York Hippodrome eclipsed all other feats of stage magic. The illusion was performed on perhaps the only stage in the world large enough for such a mammoth presentation.

A dozen men wheeled a huge cabinet onto the vast Hippodrome stage. There were curtains in front and doors at the back of the cabinet, while its floor, sides, and top were solid. The men turned the cabinet so that

its front faced one side of the stage. Then Houdini brought on a large elephant, which seemed even more enormous as it reared on its hind legs and bowed to the audience. Next, the curtains were drawn back and Houdini marched the elephant into the cabinet.

The curtains were closed again and the twelve-man crew swung the squarish cabinet around toward the audience, who could see beneath it all the time. Houdini gave the command for the elephant to vanish, the curtains were whipped open . . . and the cabinet was empty! To prove that the elephant was really gone, doors were opened in the back of the cabinet, so that the audience could see completely through.

All this took place in the middle of the stage, under the glare of bright lights. Houdini took his bow, the curtains and doors were closed, and the cabinet was wheeled off with everybody wondering where the elephant could possibly be.

The elephant, it so happened, was still inside the cabinet, though nobody was willing to believe it. All that was due to the convincing way in which Houdini, the master showman, could turn a comparatively simple trick into a near-miracle by presenting it on a stupendous scale.

The cabinet was much larger than the elephant, but this was not apparent because the immense size of the Hippodrome stage diminished everything on it, making the cabinet itself seem comparatively small. Nor did anyone note that the front of the squarish cabinet was three to four times as wide as the elephant, because it faced the side when the elephant entered.

Once the elephant and a trainer were inside, the curtains were closed and the cabinet was slowly turned frontward. Meanwhile, the elephant was being guided into a lengthwise position at one side of the cabinet, with its head toward the audience. A partition matching the black interior of the cabinet was swung into place, cutting off the sector containing the elephant, which was then completely hidden.

The space was fairly narrow at the front corner, but it widened as the partition continued inward at an angle toward the center of the cabinet, allowing first for the width of the elephant's trunk, then its head, shoulders, and finally its bulging sides. When the curtain was opened, it was loosely bunched to hide the thickness of the wall at the point of the V-shaped compartment; from there on, it was simply a matter of perspective.

The angle of the inner wall, if noted in the

blackness, simply made the cabinet look deeper. That illusion was increased when the back of the cabinet was opened. Instead of large square doors, a small circular opening was used, much like a port hole, giving the audience a clear view to the brightly lighted stage beyond. This made the interior of the cabinet seem smaller and eliminated any suspicion of a double back, which until then might have seemed a plausible solution.

The curtains were closed again and the cabinet was wheeled off by the crew before the audience could start all over in trying to figure out the mystery. For an entire season, the public continued to puzzle over the amazing disappearance, until Houdini concluded his engagement at the Hippodrome. The "Vanishing

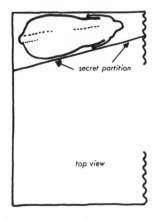

*secret partition*

*top view*

Elephant" was never taken on tour as very few theaters had stages large enough for its effective presentation.

# The Automatic Artist

The fame of the Automatic Chess Player led magicians to contrive other wonder-working mechanical figures. The public took these for genuine automata, yet they performed complex functions that seemed impossible without human aid. Like the chess player, these met with success wherever they were shown, and there was a great demand for any such figures that could be exhibited effectively upon the vaudeville stage.

One of the best of these was an "automatic artist" which performed intricate operations; yet it was so simply constructed that its mechanism could be displayed convincingly to an entire audience. The artist was a life-size figure garbed in a flowing robe with long draped sleeves. The magician first lifted it to show its light construction, then turned it sideways so it faced an easel with a blank canvas. As he wound a clockwork mechanism in the figure's back, its right arm swung upward toward the easel so that its hand rested a crayon against the canvas. Members of the audience then called out the names of simple diagrams or

pictures that they wanted the automaton to draw.

At the magician's command the "artist" traced each item perfectly, pausing after it finished each task. Between these actions, the magician removed each canvas, showed the picture to the audience, and set up another blank canvas. As a further demonstration of the automaton's ability, he told it to write certain words and numbers, which it did in a slow, mechanical fashion. Again the magician showed each canvas to the audience to prove that the mechanical figure had done its work correctly.

By the end of the demonstration, the audience was convinced that the automaton must be a human being in disguise, but the magician proved otherwise. He removed the robe and dismantled the figure, showing that it was of light construction and composed of sections like a clothing store manikin. Arms, legs and body were then packed away in a box which an assistant carried from the stage, while the magician acknowledged applause meant for the automatic artist as well as himself.

During the exhibition the magician stated that a mechanism in the body of the figure controlled a lever extending through the figure's arm. That was correct, but it did not even begin to explain the mystery of how the automaton could understand and respond to the magician's orders. The answer was it did not respond at all. Another rod extended from the body down through a hollow leg and through a small trap door in the stage. Below the stage, the rod connected with a horizontal lever that had one end fixed in a post and the other extending to an easel that duplicated the one on the stage above. A living assistant was in charge of this device, and when he heard the magician's commands, he operated the lever accordingly.

The only special mechanism consisted of duplicate springs and sockets in the body of the figure and in the device below stage, so that everything the human artist traced was copied by the hand of the automaton. Finally, at a cue from the magician, the assistant unscrewed the vertical rod, detaching it from a connection in the body of the figure. This allowed him to draw the vertical rod down through the stage before the magician began to dismantle the automaton. That done, the assistant closed the small, neatly fitted trap so that it would not be noticed.

The operation of the automaton was similar to a pantograph which artists use in copying drawings, but the principle was too well disguised to arouse suspicion of that fact.

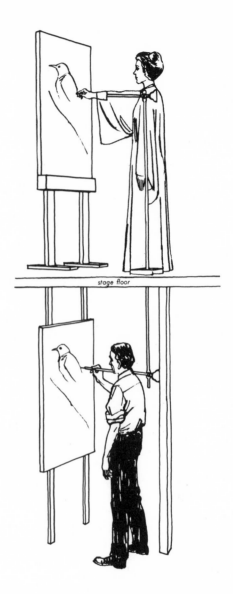

stage floor

# The Secrets of Knife Throwing

The daring and dangerous art of knife throwing can be one of the most spectacular feats of skill ever presented to the public. A girl stands against a board, her arms outstretched, while the knife thrower tosses gleaming blades at her, completely surrounding her body. The knives come so close that she cannot leave the board until they have been removed, yet the experienced knife thrower never strikes the body nor grazes his assistant.

This performance became even more dangerous as various knife throwers tried to increase the distance at which they stood from the board, thus adding to the chances of accident. The human element is always an uncertainty, and it is probable that accidents occurred in the past. As a result, a new form of knife throwing was developed. It depended on a clever trick. The performer could stand clear across the stage from the board, yet he threw every knife with expert precision. Best of all, there was no chance for a slip.

The board against which the girl stands is an ingenious mechanical device. It has a slit at every point where a knife is supposed to strike, as may be seen in the explanatory drawing. In each of these slits is a concealed knife which has a spring pivot on the point. When the girl, standing against the board, presses her arm or body at the proper spot, a knife instantly springs into view and quivers as though imbedded in the wood.

The knife thrower stands across the stage where the light is not too bright, the spotlight being focussed on the board. He takes a knife in his hand and swings his arm backward. He releases the knife and it flies off stage behind him, but he immediately flips his arm forward as though throwing the knife. So rapid is his motion that people believe he has actually thrown the knife, and they can imagine they see it flying through the air. An instant later a knife appears on the board. The whole performance is a perfect optical illusion that defies detection and the audience credits the knife thrower with mighty skill.

cross-section of board

knife after release    concealed knife

spring pivot

126

# PART 7

# METHODS *of* FAKE MEDIUMS

## Introduction

The mysteries of the pagan oracles of ancient temples, the weird wonders attributed to medieval witchcraft and demonology, the uncanny evocations by later conjurers of ghosts and visions—these phenomena find their modern counterpart in the "spirit manifestations" produced by pretended mediums. The era of the fraudulent medium began in 1848, soon after a family named Fox moved into a cottage in the little town of Hydesville, New York, only to be told that their house was supposed to be haunted.

Therefore, whenever Mr. and Mrs. Fox heard noises during the long winter nights, they attributed the sounds to ghosts. And strange noises were forthcoming; on the night of March 31, loud rappings sounded from the room where the two Fox daughters, Margaret, age 14, and Catherine, 11, slept in a double bed. The children awoke, and Mr. and Mrs. Fox called in the neighbors, who put questions to the ghost. The mysterious rapper replied by giving a rap for "yes" and remaining silent for "no."

Later, this code was amplified, and the ghost spelled words by counting to the proper letters in the alphabet. But that took place in Rochester, where Margaret and Catherine went to stay with their married sister, Leah Fish. The rappings ended in Hydesville after the girls left there, and followed them wherever they went. Allegedly, the sisters later admitted that they made the raps by snapping their toe joints, while pressing their feet against the woodwork of the bed or the floor.

Having learned that knack, they had originally planned it as an April Fool's prank on their parents and started the rapping the night before. But when everyone took it seriously, there was no getting out of it, particularly after their sister Leah guessed the secret and hired a hall in Rochester, where she took in $150 a night from gullible patrons, with Margaret and Catherine acting as mediums.

The fame of the "Rochester Rappings" spread, and the craze swept the country. Other would-be mediums learned to produce raps; and failing that, they developed new manifestations, such as table tipping, spirit slate writing, and even the so-called materialization of full-fledged ghosts. All this gained tremendous impetus during the Civil War, when bereaved parents attended spirit seances, hoping to receive messages from sons who had died in battle.

During the next fifty years, other mediums rose to fame, producing manifestations much more remarkable than those of the Fox sisters. The promise of bigger profits served as an incentive for fake mediums to improve their techniques. The trend reached its peak following World War One, when such noted persons as Sir Arthur Conan Doyle championed the cause of spirit mediums, while magicians like Houdini denounced all mediums as tricksters.

Many definitely came into that fraudulent category. A study of the methods they used during their long period of popularity forms a chapter on deliberate deception and human gullibility, as they still apply today.

# A Spirit Seance

Spirit seances vary greatly. As long as the medium simply goes into a state of semi-trance and seems to converse with spirits, there is no possibility of detecting fraud. But when physical phenomena occur, such as those produced by the Davenport brothers, there is a chance for real investigation. The manifestations actually happen; the testimony of the average witness is sufficient evidence of that. The question then is whether such phenomena are due to a natural cause, or to some supernatural agency. If the former condition proves to be the case, the manifestations are fraudulent, being accomplished by trickery. There have been phenomena which were not explained, but that does not prove that they were genuine spirit manifestations, as they may have been performed by trickery that was not detected. If they were not fraudulent, they may have depended upon a natural law that was not recognized, or which was yet to be discovered.

The burden of proof in all spirit manifestations must necessarily rest on the medium. In-

vestigators must start with the assumption that all phenomena have natural causes; otherwise their investigations cannot be accepted as conclusive. It is definitely known that fake manifestations have been produced by fraudulent mediums. Such trickery should be exposed, for if genuine phenomena do exist, then fraudulent exhibitions only hinder and handicap investigators. Following is the description of a typical fraudulent seance, conducted around a table, the fake medium being held by a person on each side.

Horns, tambourines, and bells are placed on the table prior to the seance. Each of the medium's hands is held by another person, and interlocked by overlapping the little fingers. At this point, all lights in the room are turned off so there is total darkness. The medium pretends to go into a trance and tells the two persons at his side to be sure to retain their hold upon his hands. Soon the bells and tambourines are lifted from the table, and fly around as though guided by unseen hands. They jingle and rattle from every angle, caus-

ing a terrific noise. Persons on the far side of the table are struck by the tambourines, while the horn blows near the medium. Finally the medium calls out to be released and asks for the lights. When they are turned on, the medium is found lying exhausted in his chair.

This effect is accomplished entirely by the medium, who secretly releases himself without the knowledge of the others. He draws his right hand slowly to the left, and suddenly it leaves the person's grasp. The medium tells the person not to let go, and in reaching for the medium's little finger, the person on his right gets hold of his left forefinger. Thus the medium produces the manifestations with his free right hand. Then he jerks away his left hand, and the two persons, trying to grasp it again, find each other's hand, thinking it is the hand of the medium. This, in turn, leaves him free to operate all the contrivances at once. He can swing tambourines on the ends of telescopic rods and resort to all sorts of trickery. The hands are released just before he orders the lights to be turned on and the two people will swear they held the medium until the very end of the seance.

# Spirit Table Lifting

The mysterious moving of solid objects is one of the most remarkable forms of psychic phenomena. It has occurred with many variations, among them the tilting and lifting of tables. Table tilting has been produced by many people who do not claim mediumship. A group is seated around a table, usually a light one, with their hands pressed against the top of the table. After a period of silence and concentration the table finally begins to tilt to one side, rising on two legs. It returns to normal, then tilts again, back and forth. Some mediums count off letters of the alphabet, thus spelling a word from the number of times the table tilts and stops. There are times when the table moves a considerable distance by means of a succession of rapid tilts.

This phenomenon is often the result of subconscious effort on the part of certain sitters who do not realize that they are furnishing the motive power. But actually, pressure at one side of the table can tilt up the other side a foot or more, until the pressure of people seated on that side brings it down again. Once this seesaw motion has begun, it will continue with surprising regularity. Anyone can stop such a series of tilts, if he is at the side which rises, by simply exerting considerable pressure at the proper moment, when the tilting will cease. Relaxation of this pressure will cause a new series of tilts.

Table lifting is something far more remarkable than mere table tilting. Here, the table rises completely from the floor, despite the fact that everyone is pressing at a downward angle. For this to happen would certainly require the exertion of some invisible, supernatural force, yet it seems to occur only at seances where sincere sitters are present. These seances are held in dark rooms.

The plausible explanation is that the table has been tilting so rapidly that some persons have been slow to report its action. One side tips upward and has come down again by the time an astonished sitter manages to exclaim, "This side is up!" Just then, the rotating table is beginning to tilt upward on the other side, where another sitter responds more quickly, perhaps anticipating the tilt, "This side is up, too!" Later, the self-deceived sitters agree that both side of the table must have been lifted simultaneously.

There are cases where fraudulent mediums have caused a table to float all around the room while people walk with it, pressing their hands against the top of the table. Here, the

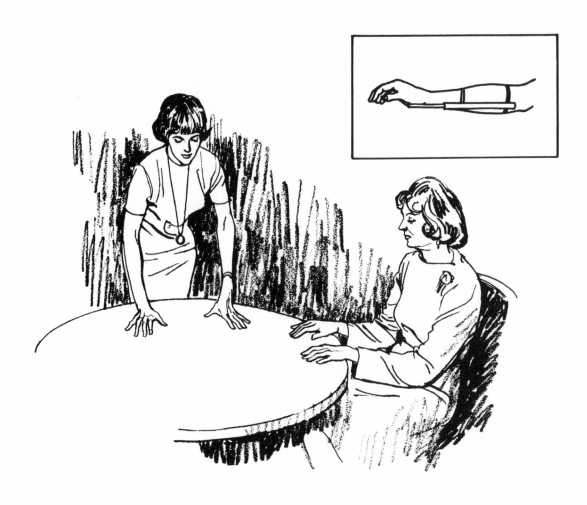

medium requires a confederate at the opposite side of the table. Each has a special tube strapped to the underside of one wrist and concealed by the sleeve. A rod comes out of this tube and extends under the table while the hand is on top. When the hands are raised, up comes the table, but it must, of course, be lifted at both sides.

Another device is worn on the belt. It is a sort of hook that swings out and engages the table beneath the top. As the sitters rise from their chairs, two of them, situated at opposite sides, have attached their belt hooks. The table rises when they get up and stays there until released.

# Spirit Raps

Ever since the Fox sisters started the "spirit rapping" craze by secretly snapping their toe joints, other mediums felt called upon to produce similar manifestations. As a result, various methods of rapping were devised, all suited to the time, the place, and the ability of the medium. In most cases, the raps seem to come from the table at which the medium is seated.

With some tables, raps may be made by rubbing the side of a shoe against the table leg, the sound carrying up into the top of the table. There are old, creaky tables that are especially suited to imitation spirit raps because of their loose joints. The medium can produce raps in a slightly darkened room by careful pressure on the table top, causing a noise like snaps to come from the table.

Sound seems to magnify in the dark, especially while everyone listens intently, as at a seance. Hence a room that is dimly lighted always helps fake raps. Noticeable raps may be produced by setting the finger tips firmly against the top of a table. The left thumb presses against the table, and the right thumbnail is pushed against the left thumbnail. This produces an audible click, and there are fraudulent mediums who have caused a succession of mysterious raps in this simple manner, without detection.

Mechanical table rappers make the best sounds, and one of the most effective types is shown in the illustration. The top of a center-legged table is hollowed out to receive an electric coil. Two wires run through the table leg and terminate in projecting points which come out of the bottom of one of the small legs. Concealed beneath the carpet, at different places in the room, are metal floor plates. Wires run from these to an adjoining room, where they are controlled by a push button. The medium takes care to place the table at one of the selected spots, and when the tiny projecting points penetrate through the carpet a connection is formed. A confederate pushes the electric button just as he would operate a door-bell, and in this manner he causes raps to come from the top of the table.

Such raps enable the "spirits" to converse

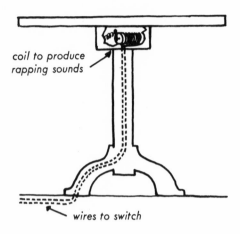

coil to produce rapping sounds

wires to switch

with the sitters who are present at the seance by code, three raps standing for "yes" and two for "no." Names may be spelled by raps which slowly count to a letter of the alphabet and then stop. Questions are asked, and these are heard by the confederate through a concealed opening between the rooms, or by means of a hidden microphone. This permits him to make the raps answer the questions intelligently.

Often the confederate is supplied with information which the medium has obtained concerning the sitter. Then the raps will spell out the names of departed persons and will give remarkable advice and information. False mediums have various means of obtaining facts regarding people who come to their seances, which makes their work very convincing.

# The Ghostly Trumpet

There are certain mediums who conduct seances using a collapsible trumpet which resembles a megaphone. The trumpet is placed in the center of the room, or taken into a cabinet. Then it begins to rise, and floats around the room while voices issue from it. If the cabinet is used, the trumpet appears from the curtains, then hovers around the

room touching the heads of the sitters. When the room is in total darkness, a luminous band is often fitted around the mouth of the trumpet so that observers can watch its mysterious flight.

At fraudulent seances, the trumpet is operated by the medium. If she is seated in a circle, she releases one hand by some artifice. If she is confined in a cabinet, she has some method of freeing herself from her bonds and getting back into them.

There are many techniques for freeing oneself from bonds, besides those employed by the Davenport Brothers. Sometimes the medium's hands are tied with a piece of stout cord having many tight knots and a length of cord running between the wrists. One of these knots is always a slipknot, and no matter how tightly it is tied, the medium can get out of it by loosening the loop around the wrist. Yet before the close of the seance, she can get her hand back through the loop and tighten the tension around her wrist.

Two secret appliances are also used. One is a long telescopic rod which the medium has concealed on her person or in the cabinet. The other is a tube of rubber hose. While in the cabinet the medium extends the rod to its full length and attaches one end to the trumpet; the rubber hose she fits to the trumpet's mouthpiece. Then, without leaving her position, she swings the trumpet out over the audience, while she speaks through the rubber hose, whispering and using false voices. The trumpet seems to float all about the room, and the "voices" seem to come directly from the trumpet.

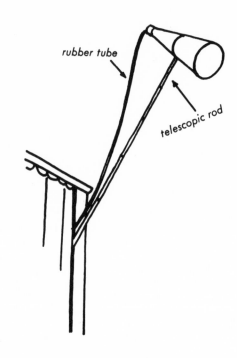

rubber tube

telescopic rod

When the luminous ring is used on the trumpet, sometimes the medium attaches the ring alone to the telescopic rod. Only the ring can be seen in the darkness, and people imagine that the trumpet is still attached to it since they do not know that the ring is removable. Thus the ring floats around the room while the medium holds the trumpet and speaks through it. This has the effect of ventriloquism, making it difficult to locate the source of the mysterious voices which are heard.

# Spirit Forms

One of the most convincing tests performed by certain mediums is the production of molds purported to be made from "spirit forms," for here is visible evidence of the presence of spirits. A pail of liquid paraffin, heated to maintain its liquid state, is placed on the floor near a circle of sitters. A pail of cool water is beside it. First the pail of paraffin is weighed with its contents. Then the lights are turned out and the audience waits for manifestations to occur. As the time passes, the spirits presumably arrive invisibly, without shape or form. When the lights are turned on again, attention is directed to the pails. On the floor are found several molds—perfect casts of faces, hands, and feet. They are supposed to have been made by the spirits to signify their presence in the room. Finally, the pail and the molds are weighed together, and the weight is found to be the same as the original weight of the paraffin pail alone. This is given as proof that the casts were made from the paraffin in the pail.

The making of a mold from paraffin is not in itself very remarkable. Plaster casts of a hand, foot, or face can be dipped in paraffin which is not very hot, and a thin film will adhere. The remarkable features of a paraffin mold seance are the mysterious production of the molds, and the fact that the weight of the molds and pail equals the original weight of the pail.

When fraudulent mediums work this trick, they have the molds prepared beforehand and conceal them in a convenient hiding place. A favorite spot is the seat of a hollow chair. As soon as the lights are out, the medium opens the side of the seat, carefully removes the molds and places them on the floor. When the lights are turned on, there are the molds. The supposition is that the molds were formed by materialized spirits who dipped their hands, feet and faces into the pail of melted paraffin, and then into the water; after which they dematerialized themselves, so that the molds alone remained!

The weighing of the molds and pail is a convincing procedure. When the pail is first weighed, the medium secretly attaches a small weight to the side of the pail that is away from observation. This is exactly equal to the weight of the molds that are in the chair. As soon as the lights are out the medium removes the weight from the pail and pockets it. Thus, the weight of pail and molds together will correspond to the original weight of the pail.

Sometimes the medium materializes "spirits" who approach the pail and pretend to dip their hands and faces in it. Then they stoop over the bucket of water and splash it about. Mean-

while, they have the molds concealed on their persons, and place these on the floor. They then vanish, but the molds remain. The appearance of facial molds is given as proof that spirits formed them.

A more convincing paraffin mold is one in the form of a clenched fist. People who know that molds can be made on the open hand are forced to admit that it would be impossible to form a mold over a bent hand and be able to remove the mold without breaking the paraffin. This trick is done by means of a rubber glove filled with water. The glove is bent in the shape desired, then dipped in paraffin. When the mold hardens, the water is poured out, and the glove can be slipped easily from the mold.

faces, hands, etc. concealed in hollow of chair

small weight

# Spirit Paintings

One of the most interesting and more recent developments of so-called psychic phenomena is the production of spirit paintings. Like many other types of manifestation, spirit paintings have been exploited by fake mediums, and the question of whether or not true paintings can be produced cannot be fully decided until the fakers have been eliminated from the field.

In a typical portrait seance, several sheets of canvas, attached to frames, are passed among the spectators for examination. One of the frames is marked, and so is the piece of canvas, to eliminate substitution. The medium enters a cabinet, canvas in hand, and after a short interim, the frame is thrust from the cabinet. If the medium has been bound, then the spectators are invited to enter. On the canvas is a finished painting of someone who has passed on to the spirit world. The paint is still damp, as from an invisible paintbrush, and the spectators are permitted to examine the canvas to identify the original marking. In the time in which this portrait was made it would be impossible for a medium or anyone else to execute a painting.

There are two methods by which paintings are produced by a medium in a cabinet. Both of these methods require a prepared canvas, but in neither case is the fraud easily detected. The secret of the first method lies in the use of a double layer of canvas, a blank piece being tacked over the sheet that bears the portrait. Since the canvas is marked on the back, it is the picture canvas that receives the identifying mark. In the cabinet, the medium quickly removes the tacks, takes off the front canvas, and replaces the tacks in order to hold the rear canvas on the frame. The blank front canvas is then concealed in the cabinet. The marks on the back of the finished picture indicate that no substitution was made, and the person who receives the portrait can take it home, if he pays the price.

The other method requires only one sheet of canvas, which has the picture on it. The painting is covered with a substance known as zinc white. The medium has a sponge satu-

rated with water or certain kinds of oil with which the zinc white can be washed off, revealing the picture beneath. In this way, the portrait will be damp when the medium brings it out of the cabinet. In the case of the double canvas, the picture may be sponged with oil as soon as the front canvas is removed.

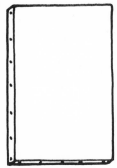

blank canvas
tacked on frame

developing picture
with sponge

# Spirit Materialization

The most spectacular spirit seances are those in which materializations are produced; for if it were genuine, a materialization would be the most convincing form of psychic phenomena possible. Seances of this type have a long tradition, dating back many years. But from the standpoint of the fraudulent medium, while a materialization may be desirable, it is extremely dangerous. Many mediums who have defied detection with trick methods have come to grief when they entered the field of materialization. Supposed spirits have been seized during many a seance and turned out to be living human beings. Police have raided the lairs of false mediums and brought back trick apparatus used in the seances. Most fake mediums now eliminate physical phenomena altogether, and materialization in particular.

In a materialization seance, a circle is formed by the sitters, two of whom hold the medium's hands, one on each side. Suddenly a glow of light appears in the midst of the circle. It grows larger and larger, and at last the luminous figure of a person stands in the circle. This spirit converses with the people, then becomes a mere glowing mass of light which finally dwindles away to nothingness. Sometimes two or three spirits appear consecutively, and a baby spirit may float over the heads of the circle of sitters. In fraudulent seances these spirits are assistants of the medium. They are garbed in white robes, painted with luminous paint which shines amazingly in the pitch-blackness of the seance room. Wearing black robes over their white costumes, the assistants remain outside the room until called in.

At the proper moment, the medium manages to release one of her hands, often with the aid of a confederate seated on that side, so that the human chain is broken. Through this break the spirit makes its entrance; and once in the circle, it draws up the black robe and begins the so-called materialization. This starts as a small circle of light near the floor. As the black robe is raised higher and higher, the figure's complete form is finally revealed, shining brightly in the center of the circle. The

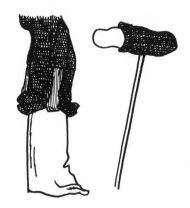

black robe is pulled down when the spirit is ready to depart.

A baby spirit is simulated by a dummy form on the end of an extension rod or pole. The dummy is coated with luminous paint and has a black cover over it. The rod, with the form, is swung around by the medium. The black cover is removed or drawn off by a thin cord attached to it and controlled by the medium or a confederate.

# Slate Messages

Perhaps the most profitable as well as the most popular form of so-called psychic phenomena was "spirit slate writing," in which messages from the other world appeared written in chalk on examined slates. As with other spirit manifestations, a medium had to be present to encourage such communications from the higher plane, usually collecting a fee or its equivalent. One slate-writing medium did a flourishing business for over sixty years, proving that this form of spiritualism was much more than a passing craze.

Because there are dozens of ways of producing slate messages, a medium can change techniques quite often when working for the same group of sitters, and clever fraudulent mediums can thus introduce new methods as fast as old ones are exposed. School slates have long gone

out of date, but some old-fashioned "spirits" refuse to write on anything else, itself an indication of trickery.

The simplest method of spirit writing requires a flap slate—a slate covered with a thin flap of metal or cardboard painted black to match the slate's surface. The medium writes the "spirit's" message on the slate beforehand and covers it with the flap, so that it appears to be an ordinary blank slate. At the time of the seance, the sitters are shown two slates, one unprepared and the other with the flap concealing the message. Both slates are cleaned and placed together, then turned over so that the flap drops from the slate with the message. In due time, the slates are separated, and the sitter finds writing on the upper slate, which is now quite ordinary. The medium sets the

lower slate aside, the flap going with it; or he may tilt it toward him so the flap drops in his lap, afterward giving that slate for examination, too.

Sometimes an already prepared slate is switched outright for an unprepared one. According to one method of practicing this trick, the medium places an examined slate beneath the table and asks the sitter to hold it there. However, near his side of the table the medium has a duplicate slate with a message written on it beforehand, held by two hooks. He simply drops the original blank slate into his lap and thrusts the hidden substitute under the table to the sitter. When, at a sign from the medium, the sitter brings up the slate, it is found to contain a message from the spirit world.

One of the cleverest and most elaborate slate-writing techniques was devised during the 1880's by the famous magician Kellar. To prove to an investigating committee that he could outdo any medium in communicating with spirits, he invited them to bring their own slates to his hotel room. There he had them make sure that nothing was under the table

before he placed one of the slates there. Kellar held the slate up against the table with the fingers of one hand, keeping his thumb on top of the table edge, while his other hand was constantly in view. Yet when a sitter reached under the table and took the slate, there was a message on its upper side!

To work this feat, Kellar had a trap door cut in the floor of his hotel room, matching the ornamental pattern of the rug. In the room below was an assistant, provided in advance with slates of every type and size. At the proper moment, this assistant opened the trap door, looked up, and saw the slate that Kellar held beneath the table. Then he wrote a message on a duplicate slate, reached up and switched it for the original, closing the neatly fitted trap when he was done.

Forty years later, Houdini demonstrated another method used by fraudulent slate-writing mediums. He placed a slate on the floor beneath a table, with a piece of chalk beside it. He held hands with a sitter across the table, making it impossible for him to write on the slate. Yet later, when the sitter himself picked

142

up the slate, he found a message on its upper surface.

Houdini's method was this: On his right foot, he wore a sock which had the big toe cut away. Under the table, he slipped his foot from his shoe, picked up the chalk with his toes, and actually wrote a brief message on the slate. That done, he let the chalk drop and slid his foot back into his shoe.

This demonstration was enacted before theater audiences, who were greatly amused at the mystification of the volunteer who had gone up on the stage to act as sitter during the slate test. The toe writing method required long practice, but it was utterly baffling, and by exposing it, Houdini clearly revealed the great lengths to which mediums would go in perpetrating their frauds.

# The Blood Writing Test

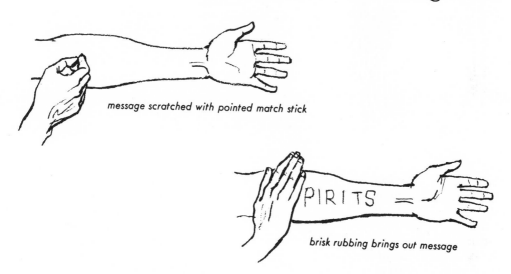

message scratched with pointed match stick

brisk rubbing brings out message

More sensational than the usual slate messages was the startling "blood writing" produced by a medium named Foster shortly after the Civil War. When he gave a seance before a small group of sitters, Foster asked them to write names of deceased persons upon small slips of paper which were folded and formed into a pile on the table. During this procedure, Foster left the table, lighted a cigar and walked about the room smoking, while people were concentrating on the names that they had written.

When he returned to the table, Foster would roll up his sleeve and show his left arm bare to the elbow, stressing that it bore no mark whatever. That settled, he let a sitter hold a folded slip. The medium then thrust his arm beneath the table, bringing it out a few mo-

ments later. There, in thin blood-red letters in the flesh itself, was the very name on the slip of paper. The sitter would open the slip and read it off, while people stared at the mysterious blood writing that could only have been inscribed by an invisible spirit hand. The writing faded soon afterward, as though erased by the same supernatural force.

Truly, here was double proof of spirit manifestations, for there seemed no other way whereby the medium could have learned the name to be selected, nor was there any other apparent cause for the writing to appear and fade. Yet the test never failed, and Foster reaped a small fortune from it before other mediums discovered his trick and began competing with him.

To learn the written name, Foster simply

switched a dummy slip for one that a spectator had written. He had the dummy clipped between his fingers and released it while pushing away the pile, at the same time picking up a bona fide slip in the bend of his fingers. While lighting his cigar, he secretly unfolded the slip in his palm and read it by the flame of his match.

If he had trouble reading the slip, he pretended that his cigar would not light, so he had to use another match. All the matches that the medium carried had specially sharpened ends, and when he turned away from the sitters, he slid his right hand up inside his left sleeve and wrote the name on his skin with the match point, pressing it very hard. By then, he had folded the slip again and in returning to the table, he pretended to pluck it from the pile at random.

After handing the slip to a sitter, the medium showed his bare arm. There was no trace of the writing on it; not as yet. However, once he stooped beneath the table, he had only to rub his left arm briefly but briskly with his right hand. When he brought his arm into sight again, the blood-red inscription was manifest. And within a few moments, it faded of its own accord.

That was the whole secret of the famous blood-writing test, though Foster was fortunate in having a skin that was particularly responsive to the process. Houdini worked it in later years, to show how fake mediums did the trick, and he added a neat twist by burning a written slip of paper and rubbing its ashes on his arm, to make the name appear.

The secret was later peddled to fake mediums for a price as low as one dollar, and with the years, it really began to get around. According to a statement that appeared in Ripley's "Believe It or Not," a twelve-year-old girl in Abbéville, France, could reply to any question by having the answer appear in bold red letters on the skin of her arms, legs and shoulders, only to fade without a trace. People attributed it to will power on the girl's part, but it sounds a lot like Foster's old trick brought up to date.

# Spirit Photographs

There are few forms of psychic phenomena that are lasting in nature. Spirit raps, table lifting, and materializations are spectacular manifestations that "spirits" are present during a seance, but these leave no evidence of the occurrence. Paraffin forms, slate writing, and spirit portraits, on the other hand, have been offered as material proof that spirits were present, since they were supposedly produced by visitors from the spirit world. However, sitters often desired to have some memento showing themselves in direct contact with the invisible spirits. It was this desire for more convincing evidence that led to the development of spirit photography, which has proven highly popular in America and Europe.

145

A spirit photograph is an ordinary photograph taken in a studio under conditions which are said to be governed by psychic influences. The photograph is a portrait of the sitter, but when it is developed, the faces of deceased persons are seen in the photograph, surrounding the sitter. This is given as proof that the spirits were present when the picture was taken. It is difficult to understand how an invisible form can be recorded by the camera yet not be seen by people who are present when the photograph is made. Although spirit photographers maintain that such a process absolutely takes place, it has been established that many of them use fraudulent methods in their seances. In fact, very few forms of psychic phenomena are so open to trickery as spirit photography.

Back in the days of the Civil War, a photographer discovered that if an old plate was improperly cleaned, and used again, a faint trace of the original picture would remain. That was the method used in the early stages of the game, but in later years spirit photographers have allowed their subjects to bring their own plates and to watch them being developed. Still the spirit forms appear, and people pay large sums for such photographs.

One neat method of producing a spirit "extra" on a visitor's own plate is by the use of a special table with a concealed electric lamp, and a developing tray with a shallow double bottom that holds a plate with small portraits already on it.

The photographer takes the sitter's picture on the unprepared plate, which can be marked for later identification. He then puts the plate in the developing tray and covers it so that no light can enter. But light does get in from below, for the medium presses a hidden release and the center of the tabletop drops in two sections like a miniature trap door. The light goes on automatically, but cannot be seen because of the covered tray.

The light causes the ghost portraits to be projected from the hidden plate in the double bottom of the tray to the sitter's original plate above. The medium presses the switch again, the light goes off, the trap closes, and the sitter's plate is removed from the tray. On the developed plate, the sitter's portrait appears with faces hovering above, dim but recognizable, like spirits.

Sometimes the faking is done with the camera itself. The photographer has tiny bits of film with faces on them. He attaches a few of these to the lens of the camera and they appear when the picture is taken. Other me-

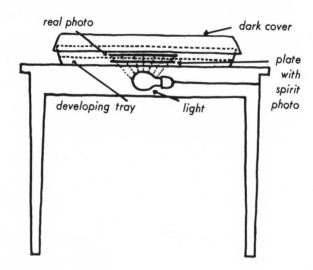

real photo    dark cover

plate
with
spirit
photo

developing tray    light

diums are adept at "switching" plates brought by a sitter for prepared ones of their own. In that case, the sitter is often invited to take a picture himself, even with his own camera, to prove that all is fair.

One keen investigator used that opportunity to turn a plate upside down while putting it in the camera. The plate had already been switched, so the spirit faces appeared when it was developed, but not quite as expected. Instead of floating above the living person's head and peering benignly downward, they were all upside down at the bottom of the picture, looking up in surprise.

Some spirit photographers have unwittingly disclosed their secrets by their own sheer nerve. One such medium offered to photograph Houdini if he would come to the medium's studio and let the medium take the picture himself. Houdini did so; and since the medium used his own camera and plate, pictures of "spirits" naturally appeared with Houdini's portrait. But

Houdini considered the evidence "inconclusive," since the photograph was not taken under test conditions. That seemingly marked the end of the matter, and Houdini died a few years later.

However, one day that same photographer took a picture of another sitter, in which the usual quota of spirits appeared. One of those "extras" was identified as Houdini, and the picture was promptly published in a psychic magazine as proof that the mediumistic photographer had brought back the great Houdini's ghost.

That caused considerable excitement, but the big sensation came when the "spirit" picture of Houdini proved to be identical in pose with the portrait of the live Houdini taken a few years earlier. The tricky photographer simply filed away the pictures of his more important client for use as spirit "extras" at a future date.